36 Hours

When disaster turns to passion

Welcome to an exciting new series of twelve books from Silhouette®, 36 HOURS, where danger is just a heartbeat away. Unprecedented rainstorms cause a 36 hour blackout in Grand Springs and it sets off a string of events that alters people's lives forever...

This month look for:

Strange Bedfellows by Kasey Michaels—
a man and a woman are trapped together overnight on a mountainside and, knowing they may never see daylight again, can't resist the taste of passion.

Ooh Baby, Baby by Diana Whitney—
a tough, wandering man plays the reluctant hero, rescues a *very* pregnant lady and delivers her twin babies in the back of his taxi!

Kasey Michaels

is a *New York Times* bestselling author who is celebrating the publication of her fiftieth novel this year. In addition to writing for Silhouette® Books, she has long been known as one of the premier authors in the field of Regency romance and mainstream historical romance. Ms Michaels was recently honoured with the *Romantic Times* Career Achievement Award for Regency historical novels and is also a recipient of the prestigious Romance Writers of America RITA Award. In fact, her career has been the subject of a Cable TV programme. Ms Michaels enjoys hearing from her readers, and you may write to her care of Silhouette Books.

36 Hours

When disaster turns to passion

STRANGE
BEDFELLOWS

Kasey Michaels

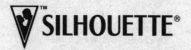

*First published in Great Britain 1999
Silhouette Books, Eton House, 18-24 Paradise Road,
Richmond, Surrey TW9 1SR*

© Harlequin Books S.A. 1997

Special thanks and acknowledgement are given to Kasey Michaels
for her contribution to the 36 HOURS series.

ISBN 0 373 65007 8

105-9904

*Printed and bound in Spain
by Litografia Rosés S.A., Barcelona*

36 Hours

When disaster turns to passion

For the residents of Grand Springs, the
storm-induced blackout was just the beginning…

Lightning Strikes Mary Lynn Baxter

Strange Bedfellows Kasey Michaels

Ooh Baby, Baby Diana Whitney

For Her Eyes Only Sharon Sala

Cinderella Story Elizabeth August

Father and Child Reunion Christine Flynn

The Rancher and the Runaway Bride Susan Mallery

Marriage by Contract Sandra Steffen

Partners in Crime Alicia Scott

Nine Months Beverly Barton

The Parent Plan Paula Detmer Riggs

You Must Remember This Marilyn Pappano

Each book stands alone, but together they're terrific!

To Marcia Evanick, friend and fellow author.
Talent always will out, love!

One

As she rounded a curve in the highway, Cassandra Mercer recognized the tall form she saw about one hundred yards in the distance.

And then she smiled, quietly deciding that there was a God—and She was on her side.

Because, after a grueling three-hour school board meeting during which her nemesis, her thorn in the side, her most blockheaded, stubborn, unreasonable parent, had once more made her life miserable by questioning her methods in the area of student counseling, she was now watching this same nemesis walk along the side of the road in a driving rainstorm.

Some might even call it a bit of well-deserved poetic justice.

"Ah," she said mockingly, her smile turning to a cheek-splitting grin even as she lifted her foot from the gas pedal. "Was that your brand-new Mercedes I saw abandoned about a half mile back, Mr. Sean Oughta-be-fitted-for-a-Frame and then *hanged?* I thought so, but I guess I just didn't believe life could be this good. Lovely weather for a long, cold, wet walk, don't you think?"

And she laughed.

The June weather in Grand Springs had been rather

pleasant when she had driven up this same twisting road on her way to Burke Senior High School that same morning. But, as she'd learned during her years living in Colorado, the weather was always subject to quick change, and June had been a more than usually damp month this year.

Wet, soggy.

But the sun had come out for a while that morning, so Cassandra had optimistically left her raincoat at home. Now, as yet another rainstorm battered against the windshield, she was beginning to rethink her joke to her cat, Festus, just this morning about building her own ark.

She slowed her Jeep to a crawl after making sure nobody was behind her, wishing Sean Frame had also optimistically left his raincoat at home. But not him. Not Mr. Perfect. He looked ready to do a speech on Being Prepared for any Emergency. Raincoat on— designer, of course. Waterproof hat jammed down on his head—at a jaunty angle, damn him. Flashlight in his hand—and the batteries worked.

Cassandra squinted through the rain and deepening dusk. "Son of a gun—he's even wearing boots. *Boots!* What else? Could he possibly also have dental floss in his pocket? Hey, you never know when you'll be lost in the woods and need to live on nuts and berries. Can't neglect dental hygiene just because you're stranded, for crying out loud. Jeez! Is it any wonder I hate this guy?"

Which she didn't, not really. Hate him, that was. She wished she could, but she didn't. He was stubborn but intriguing. Thickheaded, yet genuinely intelligent. Stern and straight-arrow, and with the most damnable way of taking her words and twisting them into something silly and shallow, but…but…

But now he was *wet*. And stranded. And being forced to walk all the way down the hill in the rain. She really should be feeling sorry for him, not vetting his appearance, trying to rationalize her mixed feelings for him. Yes. That was it. She should be feeling sorry for the handsome, infuriating rat. Okay. She'd give him some sympathy.

Poor baby…snicker, snicker.

Well, that didn't work. She still pretty much loathed the mud he was slipping and sliding in. But maybe it was the thought that counted. And, boy, was she *thinking!* She was thinking: Oh, joy. Oh, happiness. Oh, how much fun it would be to speed past the miserable man, spraying cold rainwater in her wake, maybe even tooting her horn and waving as she flashed past.

And it would serve the man right!

If only Cassandra, the sole child born to already middle-aged parents, hadn't been raised always to be nothing less than a "thoughtful, polite, *proper* young lady." A very conventional young lady. A young lady who would never, ever, even be tempted to stick out her tongue at Sean Frame and call out "nah-nah-nah-nah-*nah*-nah" as she went whizzing by in her dependable four-wheel-drive Jeep, splashing him with muddy water.

It wasn't easy being proper, but it was all she had, all she had been told to be, raised to be. The Cassandra Mercer who lived in the real world—as opposed to the Cassandra Mercer who sang and played inside her head, or the one who had rebelled, once, so long ago, for that short, terrible time—was entirely too responsible and lacking in gumption to ever *do* any of the things she was thinking.

She simply couldn't. Really.

Bummer.

Banishing her irreverent thoughts, and knowing she'd hate herself in the morning either way, Cassandra edged the Jeep forward until she was beside Sean Frame, lowered the passenger-side window and tooted her horn to get his attention.

"Need a lift?" she asked. *Drown, sucker!* her inner imp wanted to say. Clearly she was still having trouble with this Good Samaritan stuff.

And then Sean Frame, father of a wonderful if troubled young teen, and probably the main reason poor Jason was acting out in school to the point of having been put on three-day suspensions twice this term, pushed his designer-cut but now sopping wet golden brown hair out of his eyes and wiped a long-fingered hand over his handsome, wet face.

That done, he glared at Cassandra through the gorgeous, long-lashed hazel eyes the "inner" Cassandra had seen in entirely too many of her embarrassingly romantic dreams, and said, "It took you long enough, Ms. Mercer. What were you thinking as you hovered back there? Were you wondering if you could give me a small bump, pushing me off the mountain? Were you judging your chances of getting away with murdering your least favorite school board member? Or were you going to just gun the motor a time or two and then shoot past me, hoping to splash me with mud from head to foot?''

Because he was uncomfortably close to being right, Cassandra took refuge behind her twenty-seven years of experience in saying what she should say instead of what she wanted to say. In other words, she took a deep breath, reluctantly beat down the inner voice that wanted to shout back, ''Oh, yeah? Oh, *yeah?''* and proceeded to lie through her teeth.

''I haven't the slightest idea as to what you're implying, Mr. Frame,'' she said tightly, ''and can only wonder what sort of mind would think up such nonsense. I am not in the habit of picking up lone male strangers, no matter how dire their circumstances. Only after assuring myself that you were indeed who I thought you were, did I offer to assist you.''

There you go, Sean baby—now, stuff that in your nifty rainproof hat and smoke it!

''How very, um, *prudent* of you, Ms. Mercer, I'm sure. My apologies. However, I believe I can manage on my own,'' Sean said, somehow managing to look intimidating, determined, successful and too damn gorgeous for Cassandra's good—and at the same time beginning to look like he'd gone through a car wash while forgetting to bring his car.

Cassandra was tempted to take the proud, stubborn man at his word and leave him to walk the three miles to the bottom of the hill and the first service station that might still be open. Sorely tempted.

''Are you quite sure?'' she asked before he could step away from the open window.

Don't be an idiot, she meant.

"There was just a flash flood and mud slide warning on the radio," she added, to drive home her point.

If they find you dead tomorrow, I'll feel bad, she wanted to say. *Not terribly bad, but bad. After all, I think Jason might miss you. Though I'd be hard-pressed not to do a dance of joy around my kitchen table with a rose stuck between my teeth. At least then maybe I'd stop dreaming about you!*

"I'm wet and my boots are full of mud," Sean said, spreading his arms as if inviting her to inspect his long, lean frame.

She didn't think that was such a good idea. *No, thanks. I'll leave that image in my dreams, where it belongs.*

"Besides, Ms. Mercer," he added as she told her inner self to be helpful and just shut up, "I'll ruin your upholstery."

Cassandra pushed at her glasses, shoving them back up on her nose. Handsome or not, in her dreams or in her nightmares, this guy was really starting to get on her nerves.

"You can take off the boots and pay to have the upholstery cleaned," she suggested reasonably, wondering if he noticed that she was now speaking through clenched teeth. "Or are you simply afraid to be in a car with a woman who, if I remember your words correctly, 'mollycoddles students with her harebrained theories and lamentable lack of discipline'?"

Sean opened his mouth, probably to say something particularly cold and cutting. A brilliant flash of lightning was followed almost immediately by a crack of thunder that shook the Jeep. The instant increase in rain would have made a lesser man think Mother Nature had just yelled, "Hey, bozo, buy a clue, why don't you—you can't win against me!"

Cassandra hid a fairly triumphant smile as Sean closed his mouth, reached for the door handle and climbed inside the Jeep. With the door still open, he efficiently slid out of his boots and put them on the rubber mat behind the front seat, then shrugged out of his wet raincoat, revealing his expensive three-piece suit—which was still dry except for the pant legs, damn him.

She could smell his aftershave, and the tangy scent quickly traveled through her bloodstream and dissolved her kneecaps. Damn him, damn him, *damn him!*

"Are we going to sit here all night, Ms. Mercer, or had you planned to drive on anytime soon? And where were those mud slides you heard about on the radio?" he asked as Cassandra, who was now seriously considering having her head examined next chance she got, eased her foot back onto the gas and leaned toward the windshield, trying to see through the deluge outside.

"I don't know," she told him nervously as another streak of lightning split the sky. She realized she was grateful to have company for the ride down the mountain. Any company. Even Sean Frame's most disturbing, infuriating company. "The radio cut out in the middle of the warning at the beginning of the seven o'clock newscast. I think the station went off the air. And I haven't seen any lights on when I can get a glimpse of town through the trees, even though it's getting dark, so I have a feeling the power is out all through the area. There's a towel in the back seat you might want to use.''

"My car phone wasn't working, either," Sean replied. "But it never does on this section of the highway. I'll have to buy a portable one, in case I'm ever stranded without a car again. Building Burke up here farther from town where land is cheaper might have been good economically, but at times like these it's a real headache the school board should have considered. Once we're out of the hills I'd like you to stop somewhere, please, so that I can phone ahead and see what's going on. Jason might be worried."

Jason is probably hoping you'll be marooned at the high school for the weekend. And is there anything the school board did before you were on it that meets with your approval? Like, how they signed me to an ironclad contract, which has really got to twist your tail? Cassandra thought those questions, but she only said, "That sounds like a good idea. I suppose."

And then she said nothing at all, because simply driving the Jeep took all her attention—and she could only spare a small part of her brain to take in Sean's closeness, the way his towel-dried hair made him look so boyish, so human.

Human? Oh, Cassandra, her inner self tweaked at her. *Get a grip. Don't let's get carried away here....*

And then it happened. Swiftly. Quietly. Without warning. The seemingly solid wall of rock and dirt to Cassandra's left, the rock and dirt that made up the mountain drive, collapsed. Just fell.

Two

Boom, and the solid wall of mountain was gone. Like a sand castle undermined by an incoming tide.

One moment there had been a mountain wall safely straight and solid on the other side of the two-lane highway, and the next moment the Jeep was sliding sideways onto the wide gravel shoulder of the road, surrounded by a river of living mud and boulders, being swept along down the hillside as if the vehicle weighed no more than a feather.

The only thing that stopped the Jeep from moving as one with the mud and rock tumbling down the steep embankment was the strong guardrail at the side of the road, which caught and held the vehicle.

Many things happened in the first few seconds after the Jeep finally slid and bumped to a halt. For one, Cassandra realized that she was screaming, and she immediately stopped, slapping both hands over her mouth just to be certain a small, involuntary squeak couldn't still escape.

Which was a pity, because she could have used one of those hands to prudently cover her wide-open eyes, so that she couldn't look out the window and watch the whole mountain rushing past the Jeep's headlights.

Then Sean took over, exchanging places at the wheel with a numb and clumsy but still pathetically willing-to-move Cassandra, and trying to use her four-wheel drive to extricate them from their precarious position before more of the mountainside gave way and they could be swept farther into disaster.

It didn't take more than a few tense, gear-grinding, wheel-spinning minutes for Cassandra to be pretty certain that they were well and truly stuck. Hearing Sean Frame's fairly eloquent if low-pitched string of profanity as he shoved the gear stick into park and turned off the ignition nailed it down for her. Still, when she could pry her hands from her mouth, it was to hear herself ask, "We're stuck, aren't we?"

"Yes, Ms. Mercer, we're stuck," Sean answered, running a hand through his hair, then exhaling his breath in an angry *whoosh*. "If it weren't for the guardrail—but never mind that. Someone else from the meeting will be along soon enough, I'm sure."

"I—I was the last one to leave the school," Cassandra told him. "Smitty let me lock up."

He sliced her a quick, angry look. "The janitor allowed *you* to lock the school? That's not in your job description, is it, Ms. Mercer?"

Cassandra rolled her eyes, wondering if the man ever listened to himself speak. "No, Mr. Frame, it's not. But there was no reason for Smitty to be late for his dinner because I wanted to get a few files from my office, now, was there?"

He lowered his head, reaching up to rub at the back of his neck. "No. No, I suppose not. I apologize. Sometimes I come on too strong, don't I?"

Cassandra wanted to stick her little finger in her ear and give it a shake, just to clear the passageway. She couldn't have heard the guy right. "You're a businessman, Mr. Frame," she said in reply, wondering how her parents had managed to instill such good manners in their only child, when that same only child was obviously harboring a second personality, one that wanted to say, "*Strong,* Sean baby? Do the words *like a Mack truck* mean anything to you?"

A clap of thunder equal to the decibel output of five Rolling Stones concerts playing at the same time shook the mountain.

Cassandra couldn't help herself. She whimpered. "Oh, God," she groaned, then pulled her feet onto the seat, wrapped her arms around her lower legs and buried her head against her knees. "Watch for the next lightning bolt, would you? Please," she mumbled. "And then count one-one thousand, two-one thousand, until we hear the next boom, okay? I want to know how far away that lightning is."

"How very scientific, Ms. Mercer," Sean commented, then added, "or we could simply pretend that God is bowling, and the sound we hear is the pins going down? That's the fairy tale they told us at the home."

Cassandra turned her head slightly toward him and looked at him through the deepening dusk, forgetting about the storm raging outside. "The home? Are you an orphan, Mr. Frame?"

That would explain a lot. He was urbane and sophisticated, yes, but she hadn't been able to help noticing that he had this *edge* to him. It was a slightly rough edge, as if he had one foot firmly anchored in the tough but civilized corporate world, and the other somewhere to the left of success, standing in a more human, fallible, even vulnerable place.

His smile revealed straight white teeth, with one top tooth just the slightest bit crooked, showing that he'd never had braces. "And here you were, Ms. Mercer, all this time believing I'd been hatched from an egg like the other reptiles. But, no, I wasn't an orphan. Not in the ordinary sense."

She frowned. "There's an *un*-ordinary sense?"

"Actually, there is, and it's becoming more frequent all the time. You see, my father abandoned us before I was born, and my mother had this habit of forgetting where she'd put me from time to time. Unfortunately, she wouldn't give up custody so I could be adopted when I was still young and reasonably adorable."

Cassandra didn't hear the next clap of thunder, much less react to it. "That's horrible!"

"It was all right, once I got used to it. I'd spend time with her, then in the home, and occasionally, in someone's house as a foster child. It was an *interesting* childhood, and one I strove to overcome from the time I was old enough to know what I wanted. What I needed to do to get what I wanted. It was also a childhood I made certain Jason avoided. Three miles, Ms. Mercer."

"Three—oh! The lightning is only three miles away? It might as well be on top of us!" Cassandra buried her head against her knees once more, then flinched as a tumbling boulder crashed into the side of the Jeep, mashing it more firmly against the guard-rail.

To keep her mind occupied—to keep from screaming—she concentrated on the other things Sean Frame had said. She looked at him again, wishing it were darker so she couldn't see his intelligent hazel eyes, his incongruously long, lush black lashes.

"Your own childhood must have made it doubly important for you to have Jason raised in a firm family situation," she commented at last. "And yet, after allowing him to live with his mother since he was born, you've now taken total custody and moved him here to Grand Springs. How does that equate with this image of permanency you're talking about?"

He looked at her for a long moment, during which Cassandra realized that he was talking, telling her about his personal life, only to keep her mind off their current predicament, off the fact that they might, at any moment, become a part of the mountain. That was rather sweet of him—which didn't mean that she liked him. She couldn't possibly like him!

"Sally remarried about two years ago," he explained. "When Jason was fifteen. He didn't take it well, didn't care much for Bob, her new husband. And I'm pretty sure he doesn't much like the fact that there's now a new baby in the household."

He shook his head. "Sally doesn't know the first thing about dealing with teenage boys, I'm afraid, not that she was much better when Sean was younger. I tried to be there for him, but I was building my company and working ninety-hour weeks. And a child should be with his mother, or so the books say. When he ran away from home for the third time in a month, she called me in hysterics and said it was my turn. I agreed, wholeheartedly, and Jason moved in with me. Now, instead of fighting Sally's ridiculous coddling of my son, I'm fighting your off-the-wall methods, which are equally softhearted and maddening. And Jason is still—what do you call it?''

''Acting out,'' Cassandra told him, bristling. ''And now I understand why! How could you not have told me about the new stepfather? The new baby? Don't you know that these things have a profound impact on a boy Jason's age? He loves his mother, and now his mother has a new man in her life, a new child. Of course he's feeling displaced, unloved, passed over.''

''Oh, really. You should have seen his bedroom, Ms. Mercer. From the time he was born, that kid had everything he ever wanted.''

''Material things are no substitute for love. I'm telling you, he was feeling displaced, shunted aside. And then his mother goes and proves it to him by all but throwing him out of the house, straight at a man who pulled himself up from nothing and probably thinks a child like Jason is spoiled rotten and in need of a good smack upside the head to settle him down.''

''There you go—more mumbo jumbo, more textbook pap meant to—''

But Cassandra cut him off. ''God!'' she exclaimed, laying her head back against the seat as she slumped down on her spine. ''That poor kid! I'm surprised all he's done is break a couple of windows and almost fail a couple of classes.''

"Let's just hope you haven't told Jason that almost failing a couple of classes and breaking a couple of windows is permissible behavior because he now lives with his father instead of his mother," Sean shot back, reaching up a hand to jerk loose his designer tie and then roughly unbutton the collar of his designer shirt. "Or is this the new 'in' thing with guidance counselors—explaining away unacceptable behavior and placing all the blame on the parents and not the kid?"

"Mr. Frame," Cassandra began, pulling herself upright on the seat. "You have no idea how difficult it is to deal with the teenage child. I see what he does in school, yes, but unless I am informed as to his home background, his relationship with his parents, his general physical health—circumstances that are not apparent when I sit across the desk from a mulish young boy who thinks he hates everything and everyone in his life when, in reality, he is simply a painfully unhappy lump of insecurity and fear—well, it just makes my job all that more difficult, that's all."

"So you forgive him, play cheerleader, tell him to go away and sin no more, and you think you've done enough? This is your main problem, Ms. Mercer, as I've said time and again—your psychobabble methods. Where's the discipline, the punishment? When does he learn that all actions have their consequences? Surely not in Ms. Cassandra Mercer's office."

Cassandra felt her mouth open, heard words coming from it, and still couldn't believe what she said. And, to her everlasting embarrassment, the words she had said, the words that hung in the stuffy air inside the Jeep for long moments, were "You, sir, are a horse's ass!"

"That does it!" Sean shouted over the roar of the storm as he started the Jeep, slamming the vehicle back into gear and easing his foot onto the gas pedal. "Either we get out of here or I'm going to murder you," he said as he began rocking the Jeep, throwing it into reverse, pushing it into low gear—and getting them nowhere.

Cassandra was furious. "Oh, stop it! We're stuck, and that's that!"

"Damn it!" he exploded as he turned off the ignition and slammed his fist against the steering wheel before pressing his head back against the headrest. "I'd rather be in Alaska, snowbound with a polar bear!"

Cassandra pleated the skirt of her long, full cotton dress with her fingers, wondering why her anger had felt so good, why she suddenly felt so free, so liberated. Why had watching the unflappable Sean Frame lose his cool made her feel so much more in control?

Who knew?

Who cared?

She only knew she liked the feeling. "Oh, really, Mr. Frame?" she shot back, staring straight at him. "Well, I'd rather be tossed overboard into a school of hungry piranha. Or is that piranhas? Piranhi?"

He turned his head on the headrest and eyed her carefully, assessingly. She saw the way his open, sparkling-white shirt collar pressed against the side of his tanned chin, and her stomach did a small flip. "I'd rather," he bit out challengingly, "be in orbit for six months with a rabid rhesus monkey."

So, he wanted to play "can you top this insult?" did he? She narrowed her eyes, her heart pounding. "I'd rather be trapped in an elevator with an amateur rap group on their way to their first audition."

"I'd rather be locked in a bank vault with the entire Mormon Tabernacle Choir—all of them singing the Hallelujah Chorus and suffering with laryngitis."

This was fun!

"Ha! Kid stuff!" Cassandra exclaimed joyfully, then struggled for another comeback. "I'd rather— I'd rather be shipwrecked with Rush Limbaugh!"

Sean gave out a shout of laughter, then held up his hands in surrender. "You win, Cassandra. You win. Although, I must say, I didn't know you had it in you."

"Neither did I," Cassandra answered quietly, frowning at her own audacity, then smiling as she realized he had addressed her by her first name.

Then Sean waved his right hand as if asking for silence. "I think I see something moving out there," he said, using his sleeve to wipe steam off the inside of the window and peer into the now almost total darkness outside the Jeep. "Hand me my flashlight."

"Since you asked so nicely, *Sean*," Cassandra grumbled, remembering again how much she really didn't like this man, although it had been rather nice to hear him call her Cassandra instead of Ms. Mercer. But that didn't change the fact that he probably couldn't find the word *please* with half a dozen flashlights!

"Here," she said, shoving the thing at him. "Maybe it's Bullwinkle Moose come to rescue us. Because, if you haven't noticed, there aren't any lights to be seen anywhere below us, except those at the hospital. The substation must have been knocked out by the slide, considering it's only about a half mile higher up on the mountainside."

Sean didn't answer her but only cursed as he reached to roll down the window, then realized that the Jeep had push-button controls and the engine had to be engaged in order to operate them. He turned the ignition key to the "accessories" position with a determined hand, then lowered the window and stuck the flashlight outside. "There! Over there! Some nut's trying to walk out of here. *Hey! Buddy! We're over here!*"

Cassandra leaned across the seat, her chin on Sean's shoulder as they both peered into the rain and darkness. "I see him!" she shouted excitedly, earning herself a dark look from her companion. "Sorry," she added more softly. "But I do see him. If he can make it through the mud, why can't we? I mean, anything has to be better than spending the rest of this miserable night up here."

She didn't say it, but the words *with you* hung in the air, heard by them both. She took off her glasses, which she really only needed for driving—but wore almost constantly—and which were steaming up, anyway, and placed them on the dashboard.

"Do you want to take the chance of being caught in another slide?" Sean leaned his head out the window, looking down. "There's a boulder smack up against my door and the back door, holding both of them closed. Lovely dent in the metal, by the way. The road, if we could reach it from the shoulder, is nothing but a river of mud and boulders. We can't get out your side because your doors are smashed up against the guardrail. If we do get out of here, it's going to have to be through the back hatch.''

''*If* we could reach it? *If* we get out of here?'' Cassandra moved her body a little closer to his. ''Don't you mean *when* we get out of here?''

He turned his head, looking at her from only mere inches away, then put his hand on hers, squeezing it— which was the first time she noticed that she had been gripping his shoulder tightly. ''We'll get out of here, Cassandra. I promise.''

Well, as long as he promises, her inner self said, even as Cassandra tried, and failed, to relax her hold on his shoulders.

Then Sean aimed the flashlight onto the muddy roadway once more, and at the man who now stood about twenty yards away from them, obviously not able to move closer without possibly injuring himself in the debris littering the roadside. ''Do you think it's really wise to try to walk out of here, sir?'' he called over the sound of driving rain and crashing thunder.

The man waved his hands as if trying to ward off some unseen danger. ''I must go on!'' he yelled at them. ''I—I must go on!''

''What a strange reaction. Do you think he's injured?'' Cassandra asked, immediately concerned for the man. ''Do you recognize him?''

''I wouldn't recognize Jason in this dark and rain,''

Sean told her, then motioned for her to be silent while he spoke to the man once more. "I think you can make it to the Jeep if I light the way with my flashlight. You'll be safer with us until the storm's over and somebody comes to check on the slide."

"No!" the man shouted back, sounding frantic. "I must go on! There's something I must do...someone I must—I need your flashlight. Yes, that's it. Give me your flashlight! I'll send help."

Sean moved the flashlight, centering its beam on the stranger's face so that Cassandra saw the man's wet hair—it seemed to be blond, but she couldn't be sure. His eyes, however, made her gasp aloud, for they were an intense blue, and they seemed oddly vacant, as if the man was unsure of himself, of his surroundings. Which was silly, because she had never seen a more determined-looking man—save Sean Frame, of course.

The man held up his hand to block the harsh light from his eyes, took a few steps toward the Jeep, then called again. "The flashlight. Just give me your flashlight. And tell me the name of this road so I can give directions to a tow truck."

Cassandra rolled her eyes as Sean did as the stranger said, then watched as the flashlight arced through the air, to be caught by the tall, lean man with the strange blue eyes. "Well, there goes our only light," she grumbled, not knowing why she was angry. "We could have used it as a rescue beacon, you know."

"I think he'll make it," Sean said as he watched the man moving away, picking his way through the mud and boulders. "The slide can't be more than a quarter-mile wide, I imagine. Once he's free of this area he shouldn't have any problem making it to the gas station at the bottom of the hill. With any luck, we'll be out of here by morning."

Cassandra couldn't help it. She wanted to be out of here now, out of the Jeep, away from Sean Frame, away from her thoughts about Sean Frame. "Oh, really. He'll make it. But we have to stay here. That doesn't make sense, Sean, and you know it."

"Look at your shoes, Cassandra," he told her, closing the window and turning on the radio. "You can't walk out of here in those high heels, and I'll be damned if I'm going to carry you. That man, whoever he is, is only responsible for himself. I'm responsible for you, and you're staying right here. *We're* staying right here until someone comes and gets us. Now, be quiet, and I'll see if I can find a radio station that's still working."

"You're the living definition of a benevolent despot, do you know that? One man in charge of everything, and thinking he's doing his subjects a great big favor by taking care of them. I mean, Mr. Grimes could use you for show-and-tell in his European history class," she groused, silently agreeing that her shoes had definitely not been made for slogging through calf-deep mud.

And if there were another slide…?

No. She'd stay where she was. She wouldn't like it, but she'd stay.

The speakers crackled as Sean punched buttons, trying to find a working station. "You'll run down the battery unless you turn the motor back on while you do that,'' she told him, looking for reasons to hate him. ''It can get cold up here, you know, and I'd like to think we can use the heater once in a while.''

''I don't know if the mud has covered the tailpipe, but I'm fairly certain it has. Better to be a little cold than die of carbon monoxide poisoning, I've always said. It's a good thing you picked me up, Cassandra, because you never would have made it out here alone.''

''If I hadn't stopped to pick you up I'd be home right now, warm and dry and feeding Festus, who is probably starving by now and writing me out of his will,'' she pointed out, she hoped, reasonably.

''Festus? Who in hell is Festus? Ah—got one! Let's listen.''

''Pandemonium continues throughout the Grand Springs area, with Vanderbilt Memorial Hospital running on its backup generators as the blackout continues. The power outage is to blame for many accidents at intersections where the signals are not working. There have been several mud slides in the area, and motorists are urged to remain at home except in cases of emergency.

''Just a minute, folks. I've just been handed a few updates. All right. There are still several dozen people trapped in elevators around the city, so if your loved one is late tonight, don't panic—he or she may still be *stuck* at the office.

''And now, back to music. We'll give a rundown of cancellations and postponements at ten past the hour and interrupt for any updates. And please, folks, remember. It's still raining out there, and the weather center is warning of dangerous lightning and the possibility of more slides. There are no reported fatalities yet, but this isn't over. Again, please, stay where you are.''

Sean turned off the radio, and Cassandra stared at the windshield, at the dark and the rain and the continuing streaks of lightning.

''Oh, God,'' she breathed quietly, and closed her eyes.

Three

Sean switched off the ignition and sat back against the seat, his eyes on Cassandra Mercer.

He realized that he'd never looked at her before—really looked at her. He'd known her for nearly two years, both before and after Jason had transferred to Burke. They'd tangled immediately and often, also both before and since Jason had taken to destroying school property and otherwise "acting out," as Cassandra called such unacceptable behavior.

But he'd never really *looked* at her before.

She had a lovely face, actually, one that was usually hidden behind oversize tortoiseshell eyeglass frames. A flawless complexion. Her nose was small, pert, perhaps a bit audacious. And he liked her eyes—a soft brown ringed with amber and framed by long, thick, straight black lashes.

He liked her eyes. A lot.

He was certain her hair, however, would have to be considered by many to be her best feature. It was long and thick and a warm honey brown, streaked with blond highlights. A pity she always seemed to just scrape it back from her face and tie it at the nape, as if she didn't know how to do anything else with it.

Sean reached up and scratched his right cheek with his left hand, then rubbed his chin—a habit he'd had so long he didn't even wonder when it had begun—and contemplated Cassandra Mercer's mouth. Wide. Full. Quite lovely when she smiled. Not that she'd ever smiled at him before tonight.

Did she smile at Jason when she had him in for their "little talks"?

She had a long, slender neck. He hadn't noticed that before, either. But, then, he'd never seen her with her head pressed back against a car seat before, her profile brought into clear focus with each new slashing bolt of lightning, a long, thick strand of gold-streaked brown hair having escaped its prison to caress her cheek, frame her face.

Damn.

"I'm sure Frank Sanderson has everything well in hand," he said, hoping to reassure Cassandra as he faced front once more, putting both hands on the steering wheel as if ready to drive out of the mud and back down the mountain—to safety, to sanity. "He's been a good police chief."

Cassandra rolled her head to the left, and Sean felt her gaze on him. "There's someone in Grand Springs who actually meets with the grand Sean Frame's approval? Wow. Now, who was it who said there was nothing new under the sun?"

He raised an eyebrow, trying not to smile at her remark. "My congratulations, Cassandra. You've hidden your Mr. Hyde personality for two entire years. I never would have suspected you had an affinity for sarcasm—or a sense of humor. I thought you were pure Dr. Jekyll, hell-bent on solving all the world's problems through love and compassion—with several dozen off-the-wall theories about children, that have nothing to do with common sense, thrown into the mix.''

"I apologize. Being balanced on the side of a cliff, waiting for either rescue or the next mud slide must have unleashed the wild woman in me. But, to get back to what we were discussing—what would *you* do for Jason if you were in charge of his guidance and development?''

He rubbed his chin again, harder this time. ''Cassandra, I *am* in charge of Jason's guidance and development. I'm his father, remember?''

Cassandra sat up straighter in her seat. "Oh, don't be so thick, Sean,'' she said quickly, probably not noticing that his mouth opened before he quickly bit back what he was going to say. For he had decided that this was a very interesting development, watching Cassandra Mercer outside the meeting room, with nary a single copy of *Robert's Rules of Order* to get in the way of whatever she felt, whatever she had to say.

It was as if he was watching a wren metamorphose into an eagle—or Gidget turn into Norma Rae.

"We all know you're his father,'' she continued in a rush. "I'm speaking of Jason's *academic* guidance, and his social development as evidenced by his interaction with his peers and teachers. I'm here to guide Jason. That's why I'm called his *guidance* counselor.''

"How did you guide him last week, Cassandra?''

Sean shot back, getting angry in spite of himself. Besides, he felt more comfortable being angry with Cassandra Mercer. That way he didn't have to think about the fact she was wearing a particularly appealing perfume that was difficult not to notice within the confines of the Jeep. "Point out that there are bigger windows in the gym? You know, where he'd get more bang for his buck? Hey—why waste time with small windows when he could break ones that cost twice as much?"

"Now you're just being asinine!" Cassandra slapped a hand over her mouth almost before the words had escaped, her lovely brown eyes opened comically wide in what had to be shock at her own audacity. "Oh! I didn't mean to say that," she protested through her slightly spread fingers. "I'm so sorry! Really!"

"No," Sean returned quietly, shaking his head. "You meant to say it. You've probably got a sampler at home with those very words embroidered on it. You're a good actress, Cassandra Mercer, playing the caring, nurturing female and the consummate educational professional, speaking in that quiet, repressed-virgin way of yours, quoting statistics at me in meeting after meeting, your voice like water dripping on a stone as you cite sources that back up your hare-brained theories. But all the time, deep inside yourself, you're making little voodoo dolls of me, aren't you? And mentally sticking pins in them. Tell me, do you go home from school board meetings and throw darts at a picture of me you've nailed to your wall?"

Cassandra's bottom lip began to tremble, and Sean

was immediately contrite, knowing he'd gone too far, said too much. Why did this woman have this effect on him? Why did he dislike her so much? It wasn't as if she was some sort of *threat* to him, for crying out loud!

"Look, Cassandra," he began, not exactly in the mood for female waterworks. He had enough to deal with tonight, stranded here smack in the middle of nowhere, with the distinct possibility of being buried under several hundred tons of mud and rock if the rest of the mountainside decided to give way. "I'm sorry if I said—"

His apology, his plea for calm, both quickly dissolved under the warm, throaty sound of Cassandra's bubbling laughter.

"Jason is so much your son that it's almost scary!" she said as she struggled to control her giggles. "All bluster and bravado—all bristly and willing to attack at the drop of a hat in order to cover up any hurt, any pain. Voodoo dolls? Dartboards? Jason accused me of searching his locker, maybe even *bugging* it, because I seem to know too much about him."

Then she sobered. "And neither of you realize that you're both as clear as any of those gymnasium windowpanes Jason smashed. That you're both so scared and insecure and full of love that you're simply afraid to give for fear of having it flung back in your faces. You, because of your childhood, Jason because of the divorce, his mother's remarriage, even the new baby."

"That's ridiculous," Sean said angrily, but he didn't look at Cassandra as he denied her words, couldn't look at her. "Jason is spoiled rotten, and *that's* why he's a discipline problem. Sally always bribed him to be good, bought him a brand-new car the day he turned sixteen, forgave him when he started lifting money from her wallet last summer to buy CDs and new jeans, allowed him to set his own curfew. He doesn't want love, Cassandra. He wants to be left alone. He wants *his own way.* He wants to control his own life, even though he has no idea what real life even *is.* And he hates me because I took away that new car, I make him stay on a reasonable allowance, and I damn well make sure he's home at a decent hour."

Cassandra shook her head in what looked to be exasperation, and her words tumbled out quickly, as if she was thinking and speaking at the same time. "Don't you see what's wrong here? Don't you *see?* Both you and your ex-wife are teaching Jason that outlandish, unacceptable behavior is the way to privilege and material things and—even more important to him, I'm sure—what he believes should be his share of parental attention. When he lived with your ex-wife, and was bad, he got anything he wanted. Did you say this started last summer? Interesting. His grades were good until he transferred to Burke this past fall."

She shook her head, frowning. "But never mind that now. We'll get to that another time. Now that he lives with you, he may have lost some of his material things, some of his privileges, but he certainly isn't wallowing in abject poverty, and he sure as heck has gained your full attention. Do you understand now?

You and your ex-wife have been allowing the tail to wag the dog, and *neither* of you is right!''

"Oh, really?" Sean answered, feeling his jaw muscles growing tight. "So Sally and I are both lousy parents, and we're responsible for Jason's stupid behavior in school, his lousy grades. Is that the footnoted version? Will you be citing sources for me next?"

Cassandra turned sideways on the front seat, drawing her long legs up beside her on the cushion, her features animated, her eyes sparkling as another flash of lightning turned the deepening night to day. "Think about it, Sean. I talked Jason into taking early SATs—Scholastic Aptitude Tests."

"I know what SATs are," Sean interrupted. "I just didn't know Jason took them. He never told me."

"Of course he didn't! If you knew he'd had the highest score in all of Burke, you'd probably be ten times as hard on him for darn near failing two subjects this past quarter. Jason is a lot of things, but he isn't stupid! Why, he's probably smarter than you and your ex-wife and me put together. Which is why it's so terribly sad to watch him throwing all his potential away because he thinks he's so totally unloved. He's intelligent, yes, but he's still not mature enough, emotionally, to see what he's doing. But *you* are! Which is why I'm actually feeling rather glad we're stuck here—not that I want to be here much longer, of course. Now that you've told me more about Jason's background, your own background, maybe I can really make some progress with him."

She subsided against the seat once more, as if she'd

just realized she'd said too much. "If you want to, that is. And if you promise not to go running to Jason and tell him you know about his SAT scores. Because if he thinks I ratted on him, I'll lose what little ground I've gained with him this past semester, and—well…"

"You don't have to explain that one to me, Cassandra," Sean admitted, his anger draining away. "I'm very much aware of the term, and would never rat on you." Then he looked at her again, envying Jason for his ability to bring such animation, such genuine interest, to Cassandra's face. "You really like him, don't you."

Her smile lit up the night with twice the voltage of the continuing lightning strikes. "Oh, yes. He's a great kid. Funny, intelligent, inventive. But always with this underlying sense of sadness about him, you know? It's like he's this clumsy, eager, half-grown puppy with big sad eyes. I just want to hug him sometimes." She shook her head. "He'd have a fit if he heard me say *that!*"

"Yes, he probably—listen! Listen closely. Did you hear that?"

Cassandra sat up straight, turning her head from side to side, as if activating some inner radar. "Did I hear what?"

"I'm not sure," Sean said, turning the ignition key to the accessories position again and pushing the button that lowered his side window, so that he could see out into the darkness. "Some sort of *whooshing* noise…like something's on the move out there again."

And then he saw it. Saw the mountain moving, sliding toward them. Again.

"Damn it all to hell!" He closed the window, turned off the ignition and made a grab for Cassandra, cradling her body tight against his as a wall of rock and mud slammed into the side of the Jeep.

The sound went on forever. The slam of rocks, the oozing, sucking, rushing sound of ground giving way and turning to a river of mud. Boulders hit the side of the Jeep, rocking the vehicle on its chassis, grinding it against the guardrail as it lifted and began to slide downhill along with the mud.

Sean employed his long legs to brace himself against the floorboards and used one hand to pull on the headlights, something telling him that, even if they tumbled down the mountainside, maybe the Jeep's battery would last long enough to allow the headlights to serve as a beacon for possible rescuers.

If the Jeep wasn't buried ten feet deep beneath a mountain of mud.

If one of the boulders didn't come crashing into the Jeep at window level, ripping off the roof and killing the two of them instantly.

With Cassandra's head buried against his shoulder, he looked out the front windshield, watching the area the headlights illuminated, seeing the melting mountainside even more clearly with each new bolt of lightning.

They were going forward, parallel with the roadway, sliding down the mountainside toward Grand Springs one lurching, heart-stopping yard at a time, the Jeep kept upright only by the strength of the guardrail.

The screech of metal against metal, the Jeep's frame scraping along the guardrail, sent sparks into the air and turned their wild ride into a bizarre, frightening, macabre amusement park adventure.

And then he saw it. A boulder so big it was higher than the roof of the Jeep. Wider. Wedged between the guardrail and a huge, overturned tree.

And the Jeep was heading straight for it, swept along at about thirty miles an hour—or so it seemed to Sean—held against the rail like one of those tin rabbits that circle a dog-race track.

"Hold on!" he shouted over the escalating noise…the rush of rain…the rolling thunder that slammed and reverberated inside his chest…Cassandra's single scream, which cut straight into his heart.

Four

It was like a head-on collision with a brick wall, and the hood of the Jeep folded up like an accordion even as Sean threw himself across the front seat and on top of Cassandra, knowing he had to get himself away from the steering wheel, which could otherwise have ended up halfway through his chest.

He stayed very still, trying to decide if they had reached the end of this latest storm-induced journey, listening to the relative quiet that followed, watching for lightning, then silently counting one one-thousand, two one-thousand, just as Cassandra had suggested.

Yes, the rain was beginning to slacken off.

Yes, the storm seemed, at last, to be moving away from them.

But the mud remained, and the danger was still with them. There could still be another slide.

Slowly, he began to realize that Cassandra was lying quietly beneath him—quietly, but with her arms wrapped around his back in a death grip, her body pressed against his, her teeth chattering.

"It's all right, Cassandra," he breathed quietly, soothingly, whispering the words through the tangle of her hair, his lips against the warm skin of her ear. "It's all right. I promise."

She swallowed. Once. Twice. He could feel the movement of her throat, sense her fear, hear the small catch in her throat as she took several deep, steadying breaths. "Just hold me, all right?" she asked after a moment. "Please. Just hold me. Keep telling me it's going to be all right."

The smell of her perfume teased at his nostrils. The warmth of her body, fitting so perfectly against his, set off warning bells in his head. She held on to him with all of her strength, all of her desperation, all of her very reasonable fear.

Because they could die out here. One more large slide and the guardrail was sure to break away, or they'd be buried alive under the mud and boulders.

He knew it. She knew it.

And lying to her, saying everything was going to be "all right," didn't mean squat.

She probably knew that, too.

He pressed his lips against the side of her throat, tasting her, trying to soothe her, divert her attention away from what might be the inevitable tragedy that awaited them. "I'm here with you, Cassandra. I won't let anything hurt you."

God! She felt so good. So alive. And he needed to feel alive.

He allowed his mouth the liberty of another kiss, and then another, tasting the sweet skin of her throat, easing himself backward slightly, moving his body lower along the length of her, so that he could lift his head.

Lift his head…and look down at Cassandra as she lay against the seat, her hair now loosened from its ridiculously severe style to tangle in a golden softness around her head, to frame that so vulnerable, so unexpectedly beautiful face.

Lift his head...so that he could watch Cassandra's face as the now infrequent lightning gifted him with enticing glimpses of her doelike eyes, her clean, flawless sweep of cheek, her full, trembling mouth.

Lift his head...so that he could attempt to read her expression, gauge her level of fear, be comforted and aroused by the trust he saw there, her willingness to believe he was there for her, wouldn't leave her, would never, ever leave her.

Lift his head...then lower it to find her mouth.

White-hot lightning exploded behind his eyes, a thunder he'd never heard before shook his entire body with its intensity.

Her mouth was warm in the damp coolness of the night. Her body, a blast furnace giving off the heat he sought, the heat he needed. It was the life force he so desperately required to prove that he was alive, that she was alive, that they both would survive, and would not possibly perish here on the side of a mountain.

The first seconds of tentativeness quickly gave way to a fierce intensity that had him slanting his mouth against hers again and again, pressing her head back against the cushions as her full lips opened, allowing him to deepen the kiss.

She didn't move to push him away. Her arms tightened around him, drawing him closer, even as he realized that his hands were on her body, finding her, molding her, learning her lush beauty through the camouflage of her business suit. The crisp white blouse seemed to disappear beneath his oddly fumbling fingers.

It was all so Harry High School, his brain warned him. So crazy. Making out in the front seat, frustrating himself with kisses and petting and long hours of unfulfilled sexual longing. The steering wheel jamming into his thigh, the chrome door handle only an inch from his head, his suit jacket twice as difficult to remove than his letter sweater had even been.

But he couldn't stop. And Cassandra didn't want him to stop. Not when she had somehow undone the buttons of his shirt, not when she was even now pressing kisses against his neck, his bare chest.

They didn't speak, for there were no words. There was only this strange urgency, this need to feel alive. To give. To take. To share.

To keep the bogeymen away...

She was silk beneath his fingers, fire burning his flesh. He unsnapped her front-closing bra, a small part of his brain amazed by the feminine beauty of her undergarments, the lace and satin she hid beneath her business suits and long, shapeless cotton dresses.

He pressed the flat of his hand against her slightly concave stomach, then found the lacy band of the slight wisp that eased so satisfyingly down her thighs, over the thigh-high stockings that were another vague, marvelously unexpected surprise.

This was a woman who was innately sensual, no matter how she strove to show the world her professional front, her businesslike facade.

And it all had been there, in her eyes, all along. He

simply hadn't seen beyond the tortoiseshell glasses, the scraped-back hair, the image she so carefully projected. She hid behind her glasses, her clothing, her professional exterior, the sources she quoted, the terms and theories and statistics—and all the while wearing underclothes that were designed to drive a man out of his mind.

Why? his brain asked even as he dipped his lips into the soft indentation of her waist, sliding his tongue along the path his hands had taken, even while listening to the soft whimpering moans Cassandra breathed out with each shallow breath.

I don't care why, another part of him answered dismissively as she cradled his head between her hands, possibly to stop his downward investigations, possibly to urge him on to this greater intimacy.

He kissed her belly, the silky insides of her thighs above her stockings, the curve behind her knee.

He ran his hands along her flaring hips, teased his way across her lower stomach, then nervously slid his fingers between her legs, feeling her tense against him, then slowly relax her tight muscles as her hips lifted off the seat, as her legs fell open, as she allowed him to explore her deepest secrets.

Only when he moved to replace his fingers with his mouth did she pull away from him, her eyes still tightly closed as her head pressed back against the passenger-side door, and she held out her arms to him, urging him to hold her.

Because she needed him. Needed him close, needed an anchor to keep her from spinning off the mountainside, possibly off the earth entirely. Yes.

That was how he understood her actions, and her next words confirmed what he had thought.

"Please," she whispered brokenly, her tone seemingly caught between passion and unexpected embarrassment. "Please, Sean. Hold me. Hold me."

He silently cursed the confines of the front seat, wishing he'd had the foresight to move them both into the wider back seat, but he was suddenly afraid that any hesitation, any conversation at all, would not only shatter Cassandra's mood, but Cassandra herself.

So he did just as she wished, lowering himself against her, his hand never losing contact with her, never lessening its sweet assault.

He kissed her breasts, rubbing his tongue over her nipples, kissing her, nuzzling her, his breath leaving him in a long sigh as she wrapped her arms around him once more, her body once more turning liquid, willing, eager.

He took her mouth again, hungry for her, feeding on her, finding his life through her, clinging to life even as he knew it could slip away at any time, reaffirming her existence and his own.

Simple. Elemental.

Man. Woman.

Life.

She was ready for him. And he was oh-so ready for her. To bury himself within her warmth. To feel the pulse of life between them. This beautiful, unreadable, unfathomable, intriguing, exciting woman. He wanted her. Had to have her. Might always need her...

And then he felt the barrier between them. Sensed

it. Realized that she was once more tense, holding her muscles tight even as she continued to cling to him, continued returning his kiss.

Could it be? Was it possible?

"Cassandra, are you sure…?" he murmured questioningly against her lips. Blood drummed in his ears, trying to block him from thought. But he was no raw high school jock experimenting with sex, and she was no giggling, willing cheerleader.

Was this possible? Was this real? Was he actually in the front seat of a Jeep poised to roll down a mountainside—ten feet from a particularly unpleasant death—with a *virgin?*

God surely had a lousy sense of humor….

"Please," she whispered against his ear as she tore her mouth away from his, then buried her head against his shoulder and neck. "Please, Sean. I want this. I truly want this. I—I shouldn't have to die without…without *knowing.* Please!"

And then, of all the craziness that had happened that night, Cassandra did the craziest thing of all—or at least that's how Sean viewed it.

She held on to him tightly, her head raised from the seat to press against his shoulder.

And she began to move.

Move her hips, her whole lower torso. One long, silk-clad leg snaked up and over his thigh, slid up onto his back, holding him to her, imprisoning him, urging him on, helping him, aiding and abetting him.

And he was lost.

The barrier disappeared, broken by passion, by a need that made his throat raw, choked off his breath,

and he was sheathed in her warmth—fully, completely.

His heart was going to burst, he knew it.

His brain had already exploded, leaving all reason to vaporize into the night air without a trace.

She was his, and he took her. She was life, and he reveled in her. She was heat and passion and promise. Together, they moved. They melded. They soared. They left the mountainside, their precarious position against the guardrail, and entered into a world so basic, so natural, that nothing else existed, nothing else mattered.

Five

"Are you all right?"

Cassandra silently considered the question. Was she all right?

That would depend.

Was she all right as compared to not being all right? As compared to being what she had been approximately five minutes ago? As compared to being alive now after twenty-seven years spent merely existing?

"Yes. I think so," she answered at last, keeping her head averted as she tucked her blouse into the waistband of her skirt. "How are you?"

"Me?"

He sounded uneasy, maybe even chastened. Did anyone use that word anymore—chastened? She doubted it.

"I'm fine. A little afraid that I've just taken advantage of you. A little stupid that I'm not as prepared for impromptu sex as I was back in my high school and college days. We do have to talk about that, you know. If we live through this, that is."

Cassandra shoved her fingers through her hair, trying to tame it, then confined its length once more in the elastic band she'd found on the floor. How had it gotten on the floor?

Better question—how had her bra come to be hanging from the rearview mirror?

"If we live through this, that is," she repeated hollowly, looking out through the passenger-side window and seeing nothing but an eerily quiet black night. "What time is it?"

"Nearly midnight," he answered, pushing the button on the side of his watch that illuminated the dial. "The rain stopped about an hour ago, after the second time we—"

"Oh. Yes. Well. Um—here's your tie. It was on the floor, um, under my shoe."

Cassandra felt heat rushing into her cheeks and averted her head once more even as she felt the tie slide through her fingers. It had been bad enough that she'd so lost control of herself that she'd allowed Sean to make love to her a single time.

But a second time? And *she* had been the one who had initiated that second time by her seeming inability to stop kissing him, stop holding him, stop wanting to feel again what she had felt so briefly after the rising passion and that strange, fleeting moment of pain.

And the second time had been better. Sweeter. Longer to reach. More solidly held. Incredibly intense. Leaving her boneless, breathless, and aware that she had never before been so shattered, so whole.

She felt sore between her legs now, but not a hurting sort of sore. More of an awareness, an oddly pleasurable feeling, actually. Even comforting. And wonderfully reminiscent of what had happened to cause this unique new awareness.

But she didn't want to talk. Couldn't face a post-mortem right now. Besides, they'd only find some way to fight about what had happened, just as they always seemed to strike sparks off each other. Although, she considered wildly, biting on her bottom lip to keep a silly smile from forming, their next parent-teacher conference ought to be a real corker!

Stop it, Cassandra! she screamed inside her head. *Just stop it!*

Sean didn't say anything, so she decided he was as conflicted as she was at the moment. They had thought they were going to die, so they gave in to impulse. That's all it had been.

Studies had been done on this subject, she recalled, showing that humans placed under considerable strain, made to live through life-and-death situations, often responded with the basic, biological forces that urged them to reaffirm their existence by exercising their powers of propagation, hoping to make themselves immortal by the simple sexual act, which validated their existence and was meant to continue the species.

Or some such stuff...

But what if they *didn't* die here on the mountainside? Now, there was a thought worth exploring! She had been so terribly afraid to die, so angry that she had barely begun to live, to experience. Now she was worried that they *wouldn't* die? That they'd live to face the consequences of their actions?

Wasn't that a kick in the head!

"Um—Sean?" she said, talking in order to stop the ridiculousness going on inside that same kicked head. "Do you think the radio still works?"

"It could still be in one piece, I suppose," he answered, shifting his body so that he was almost behind the steering wheel that had come forward into the driver's side of the car. He was moving himself away from her, which she appreciated greatly, as it would probably be easier for her to breathe once there was some physical distance between them. "The steering column is slightly bent, but it's possible."

He turned the key in the ignition, and a moment later was rewarded with the sound of a reporter's voice coming to them from beyond the darkness:

"...just a short while ago without ever really regaining consciousness. Mayor Stuart, whose death has been tentatively attributed to a heart attack, is the only casualty so far tonight, and her death is not now considered to be storm-related.

"Road crews are already working to clear three mud slides in the area, concentrating their efforts now on opening the road to Burke Senior High School after learning that school board member Sean Frame, a local businessman, has not returned home after a meeting there earlier this evening. We'll be back after this word from Randolphs—home of fine dining in Grand Springs for—"

"Jason must have reported me as missing," Sean said after he'd switched off the ignition. "And here I thought he'd be throwing a party."

Cassandra blushed again, remembering her earlier sarcastic thoughts about Sean's possible disappearance, and memories of kitchen tables and dancing and that business about a rose between her teeth.

My, how a few hours—and sexual intimacy—could change the way you thought about a man. That, and listening to how Sean Frame had grown up, what had made him the man he was today, and why he treated his son the way he did. Learning how very much he loved his son.

"I guess Festus didn't know I've got 911 on speed dial," she said, trying to joke and wincing as she heard what she'd said.

"Festus. Yes, you mentioned him before. I take it this is your dog?"

"My cat, actually."

"Why did you name him Festus?"

"Because I didn't want to name him Jack?" Cassandra winced again. Boy, was she edgy! "I'm sorry. I named him Festus because, well, because he just *looked* like a Festus. Kind of scraggly and pathetic. Although, that was when I found him hanging around my garbage cans. Now he's fat as the Cheshire cat and twice as lazy. Must weigh at least twenty pounds, and eats me out of house and home. Why he—" She turned to look at Sean. "Am I babbling? I think I'm babbling."

"You're babbling," Sean agreed, reaching out to take her hand. "So, because you're babbling, we won't talk about anything else tonight. Agreed?"

Cassandra released her breath in a short, quick rush. "Agreed."

"But you *could* be pregnant, you know."

"Oh, for crying out loud!" Cassandra exploded,

pulling her hand away from his. "That only happens in bad books and even worse soap operas."

"And in the back seat of a really fantastic '68 Chevy Malibu with bucket seats and four-on-the-floor—which made the back seat a necessity rather than an option. If you don't believe me, you can ask Sally."

"Your ex-wife?" Cassandra knew she asked the question, but her voice was so low that she barely heard herself speak. Probably because she didn't want to hear his answer.

"My ex-wife," he repeated, and she could hear the regret in his voice. "Young and dumb, that was us. But we did the right thing. And we got Jason out of the deal, which made it all worth it."

Cassandra didn't know where to look, how to sit, what to say. Her hands fluttered in the air, then settled once more onto her lap. "I'm not pregnant. I couldn't be pregnant. That's—that's just impossible."

"You're on the pill?"

"No." She tried to swallow, but her mouth was dry.

"You're infertile?"

She shot him a quick look. "How on earth would I know that? I was a virgin, remember?"

"My point exactly," he continued, sounding less like a human being and more like a finely oiled business machine with every word, his tone tight, his lips tighter. "So, until we have evidence to the contrary, Cassandra, I think we should consider the possibility that we'll be married within the next six weeks—no matter how much neither of us likes it. Do you understand now?''

"Oh, yes. I understand. Unlike your son, you're one responsible son of a bitch, aren't you?'' Cassandra closed her eyes, laying her head back against the seat. "So, tell me, if we rock it really, really hard, do you think we can get the Jeep to roll off the cliff?''

Six

Sean watched as Cassandra was wheeled off to a cubicle in the emergency room, an ice pack on her ankle. It was eleven in the morning—almost an hour after their rescue from the Jeep.

They'd done so well—up until the last moment, when she'd stepped on a slippery rock and twisted her ankle. No more than another ten or so yards to the road maintenance truck and safety, his arm around her waist to help her keep her balance, and she'd slipped. He had managed to keep her upright, but the damage had already been done.

What if her ankle was broken? Wouldn't that just be the capper to what had become the longest, strangest night of his life?

He scratched at his cheek, then rubbed his chin, feeling the dried mud on his face. Well, at least she had stayed upright. He, on the other hand, had only managed to hand her off to one of their rescuers before he'd lost his footing and landed on his backside, sliding a good twenty feet downhill before coming to an ignominious halt. "Sean!" she'd called out in a frantic scream as he slid back toward the Jeep, and the guardrail, and the long drop off the side of the mountain.

Some hero he was. Sitting here caked with mud from head to foot, his suit ruined, his shoes gone. Wet and shivering in a blanket someone had given him.

"Are you sure you're all right, Mr. Frame?" one of the nurses asked him, handing him his third cup of hot, strong black coffee. What was her name? Katey? Kitty? Yes, Kitty. "I'm fine, thank you, Kitty," he answered, then proceeded to scald his tongue with his first sip of the steaming brew. "You contacted my son?"

Kitty smiled and nodded, just as if the reception area of the emergency room wasn't crowded with patients waiting to be seen, all casualties of the storm. "He's coming right over. He said something about having to first hunt around and find the keys to your Blazer, as his own car had been stolen. Your luck certainly hasn't been very good lately, has it, Mr. Frame?"

"Cute kid," Sean grumbled under his breath as the nurse turned away to answer a question directed at her by another patient, who was holding a bloodied cloth to a gash on his forehead. "Not a stolen car. I *sold* the car." He took another, more cautious sip of coffee. "Probably one and the same thing to Jason."

Thoughts of his son took him back to thoughts of Cassandra, about their hours together on the mountain, about the possible consequences of those actions. It was amazing. He'd pulled himself up by his own bootstraps, built himself a damn fine business, and still acted like an eighteen-year-old when presented with a dark night and a conveniently isolated place.

Except that he wasn't eighteen anymore, and Cassandra Mercer was a far cry from his ex-wife. For one thing, he didn't much like Cassandra Mercer. Or so he'd thought when he was driving home from the school board meeting a lifetime ago, still smarting from her rational, sanely delivered, hopelessly technical explanation of the rudiments of modern guidance counseling when applied to the teenage boy.

It had been Cassandra, not he, who had saved Jason's backside from starting off the fall term with another school suspension. She had convinced the other members of the board that her way was better than Sean's way—which had a lot to do with "don't do the crime if you can't do the time."

She had even arranged a summer job for Jason, so that he could reimburse the school for all damages. She'd set up meetings with him over the summer, where he would hand in reports and essays on subjects ranging from Vandalism, through My Favorite Person, to—for crying out loud!—the History of Glazing.

Cassandra Mercer had taken on Jason as her own personal responsibility, and she was undermining Sean's own position as the boy's father. It was that clear, that simple. But she didn't see it that way. The rest of the board didn't see it that way. And they'd allowed her everything she'd asked.

Making him look like a fool, like some sort of heartless ogre. Which he wasn't, damn it!

Was he?

And now—now that he and Cassandra *had* spent those hours together in the Jeep—now what? Bedding a virgin did *not* come under the heading of casual sex. No way. No how. He didn't know why she'd allowed him what she'd allowed him. He didn't know why he'd so lost his head as to find himself kissing her, holding her, feeling as if he would never, ever want to let her go.

Don't lie to yourself, Frame. It's counterproductive, his inner self warned. *She wasn't the same Cassandra Mercer you've been locking horns with these past two years, the same Cassandra Mercer who's gone and stuck her fairly remarkably enchanting nose into your personal relationship with Jason this past year. That was a whole new Cassandra Mercer you were with last night. Bright. Funny. Sexy.*

Where had she been hiding this surprisingly adorable, human side of herself for the past two years? And another thing—*why* did she feel it so damn necessary to hide? Like with that silk underwear? Not that anyone would want a high school guidance counselor to dress as if she was only passing through the school building on her way to a cocktail party—but did she really find it necessary to hide under severe business suits and shapeless dresses?

Who was the real Cassandra Mercer? The competent career woman, or the fairly smart-mouthed silk-and-lace temptress he'd discovered last night?

And why did he feel it to be vitally important to him, maybe even critically essential to him, to find out?

Because she could be pregnant?

Sean shook his head. The chances of that sort of lightning striking twice in one man's lifetime had to register somewhere between slim and none. It was in the realm of possible, but not probable.

But he was going to stick to the woman like glue until he knew, one way or the other. Whether she liked it or not.

Because you want to get to know her better. Because you never, ever felt what you felt tonight, wrapped in her arms, hearing your name on her lips. Because she's intriguing, and loving, and loyal, and—

"Oh, shut up!" He ground out the words, shaking his head, shaking away his thoughts.

"Pardon me? Did you say something? It's just so noisy in here, isn't it? Hard to believe there's so much noise in a hospital, but then, as I always say, if you want a good rest, last place you'll ever find it is in a hospital. Mind if I sit down?"

Sean looked up in time to see a heavy-set, middle-aged woman dressed in a flowered muumuu and mud-caked sandals collapse into the chair next to him, letting out her breath in a long *whoosh.*

"What a night!" she said, turning to look at him. "My son-in-law broke his arm trying to help pull some fallen branches off the roof. The roof! What was he doing on the roof in the middle of a storm? Now, I ask you, is this stupid, or what?" She shook her head. "What Mary Lou ever saw in that boy is totally beyond me."

She shook her head again. "Terrible about the mayor, isn't it? You suppose they still have her here? They brought her here to Vanderbilt, you know. I heard it on the radio."

"Really," Sean said, not eager to start a conversation with the woman, but wondering if she knew more than he'd been able to hear on Cassandra's car radio. "I understand it was probably a heart attack."

The woman nodded sagely. "Yup. That's what I heard, too. Funny, she didn't look the type. Now, me—" she spread her arms, calling attention to her girth "—I'm a prime candidate. Taking care of my own house, taking care of Mary Lou and her husband the tree surgeon, watching all three kids while they both go out to work. Well, it's a wonder I haven't dropped over half-a-dozen times. And how about that Sloane girl? The one trapped somewhere in a mine or a cave or something? I'll bet her parents are going crazy right now. Lord knows I'd be a basket case."

"They haven't found her, then?" Sean asked. He'd heard the news on the radio on the way to the hospital. The young girl had fallen into a cave which had been unearthed by a mudslide. Silently Sean agreed that he, too, would be out of his mind if Jason were caught somewhere in this storm. Kids. They broke your heart, no matter how you looked at it.

"Oh, they've found her. They just can't get to her, that's all. The police have been begging for volunteers all morning. You know, people with earth-moving equipment and the like. They'll get her. It's just a matter of time. Hey—didn't they say her mom's a doctor? Is she here at Vanderbilt, do you suppose?"

"Yes, yes, I believe she is, as a matter-of-fact," Sean answered as the electric-eye doors to the reception area opened and Jason walked in, shaking rain from his dark brown, chin-length hair. "That's my son. If you'll excuse me?" he asked politely, already rising and waving to get the young man's attention. "Jason! Over here!"

Jason scanned the crowded reception area, frowning, then grinned as he caught sight of his father and edged his way through the crowded room to stop in front of Sean. "Wow!" he exclaimed, grinning. "What did you do, Dad, bodysurf down the mountain? Jeez, you're a mess!"

Sean opened his mouth, a sharp retort ready—comparing his own appearance to that of his son, who was wearing cutoff pants with the crotch hanging nearly to his knees and a Dead Head T-shirt—and then smiled. He might not have ever seen his son again. "Yeah," he said instead, grinning at the kid, "but you oughta see the other guy."

Jason's smile slipped a little, then broadened with both delight and surprise, and Sean mentally kicked himself, realizing that his son had been braced for yet another tense confrontation. About his clothes, about his hair, about his attitude—about anything Sean could find to complain about, criticize.

"But you're okay, right?" Jason asked, trying to be flip, but sounding very young, still a little scared. "When you didn't come home, and then I heard about the slides—" He broke off, shaking his head.

"You reported me missing, didn't you, son?" Sean asked, and Jason nodded. "That was a very responsible thing to do. And you may have saved my life. Mine, and Ms. Mercer's."

Jason's head came up, and he quickly looked to his left, to his right. "Ms. Mercer? She was stuck up there, too? Is she all right? Where is she?"

A pang of something very close to jealousy shot through Sean as he realized how very much Jason must like Cassandra Mercer. How very much she liked him. And how very much Sean was standing on the outside, looking in, with the both of them. "She overturned her ankle as we slogged through the mud to the maintenance truck. They're looking at her now."

"But she'll be all right?" Jason asked, obviously needing further proof. "I mean, she's okay. Not really hurt or anything." He clapped his hands together a few times, looking over his shoulder and toward the door to the treatment areas, fidgeting where he stood. "Is there anyone we can ask? Anyone who knows anything?"

This, Sean thought with a sudden burst of insight, *is a boy with a man-size crush. And it doesn't take a brain surgeon to know that Jason would be one ticked-off kid if his father tried to move in on what he considers to be his territory!*

"She's fine, son, honestly. In fact, she rescued me. My car was an early casualty, and Ms. Mercer picked me up in her Jeep just before the mountain slid down on both of us. I'm just glad we could keep each other company until we were rescued. I have to tell you, it was pretty hairy up there for a while."

"Uh-huh," Jason mumbled, ignoring him, still glancing toward the double doors every few seconds. "We can take her home once she's done here, right? I mean, there's still no lights on anywhere in town, and if her Jeep is still stuck up there…?"

He turned back to Sean, who could see the gears

working in his son's head. "Or I can take you home now, and come back for her? You know, if you don't want to wait? Yeah, that would be good. You need a shower and everything, and I can take Ms. Mercer home, help her into the house, check on Festus—you know."

Sean was no longer amused, if he ever actually had been. "You've been to Ms. Mercer's house before this?" he asked, trying to keep his tone neutral, casual.

Jason's eyes became shuttered, his chin coming up in a belligerent, all-too-common sign Sean had long ago learned to dislike. And dread. "Yeah, I have. Lots of us go to visit her. We sit around, eat stuff she makes, watch dumb movies, maybe help her cut the grass or something. So what?"

"So," Sean returned, trying to be careful, yet knowing he was getting angry, "it's not exactly usual for teachers and students to interact quite so, um, *closely*. That's all, Jason, nothing more."

"Yeah? Well, she's not my teacher, okay? She's my guidance counselor. What are you gonna do now, Dad—turn her in to the rest of your school board gestapo? Jeez!" Jason rubbed a hand across his mouth. "You know, I don't know why in the hell I bother trying to—"

"Don't swear, Jason," Sean warned tightly. "I'm not half as impressed by teenage profanity as your friends might be. Now, settle down, all right? We'll wait here together and make sure Ms. Mercer gets home."

"Oh, yeah? Well, I'll be waiting outside, okay?"

Jason announced, stomping off before Sean could answer him, and then easing into what he must have thought was a "cool shuffle" when he turned the corner at the end of the row of chairs and headed for the door.

"Kids are such a blessing, aren't they?" the lady in the muumuu said, laughing. "Makes me wonder why I didn't just raise dogs and be done with it. Don't have to send them to college, either."

Sean looked at the woman, saw the laughter in her eyes, saw the camaraderie of shared experience and smiled his agreement. "No, just obedience school. Which my kid flunked out of last year, I think."

She nodded in understanding. "Mine were all Sesame Street dropouts, as I always tell them. But they do grow up, hard as that is to believe sometimes. And then they marry bozos who climb up on a roof in the middle of a storm. Hey—is that who you're waiting for? That pretty thing over there, on the crutches?"

Sean leaped to his feet, nearly tripping over his dragging blanket. "Yeah. That's her," he said, wishing Cassandra didn't look so small all of a sudden, so vulnerable.

"No wonder the kid's got a crush on her," the lady said, shifting her bulk in her chair. "Just like his daddy. Good luck to you. I think you're going to need it."

"Yeah. Thanks," Sean answered automatically, then realized what the woman had said. He turned back to look at her. "But you're wrong. I don't have any feelings for the woman one way or another."

She wrinkled her nose. "Of course you don't. Now,

you just go on believing that. Her name's Mercer, right? I think that's what your son said. What's yours?''

"Frame," Sean answered, automatically polite. "Sean Frame. Why?"

"Because I'll be watching the wedding announcements, that's why. I've got a sixth sense about these things, you understand. Now, go on. I don't think she's quite got the hang of those crutches yet."

Sean thought he probably should say something else to the woman, offer some sort of denial, but he honestly couldn't find the words. So he just said, "Thank you and good luck with your son-in-law," and went over to intercept Cassandra as she headed straight past him, toward the doorway and the street outside—just as if she could get home on her own.

"Jason's outside, waiting for us," he said without preamble as he tried, without success, to put his hand on Cassandra's back, to help her as she balanced crutches and the purse she had slung over her shoulder. "We'll take you home. It's not broken, is it?" he asked then, indicating her heavily wrapped ankle with a wave of his hand.

"No. It's just a slight sprain," she told him, most of her concentration on maintaining her balance. "I just have to keep my foot propped up for the weekend." She sliced him a look out of the corners of her eyes. "Doesn't that itch?"

"What? Oh, you mean the mud? No. I don't mind it," Sean said, then realized he was scratching his cheek again. "But I wouldn't turn down a long, hot shower. Only the power is still off all over the city, which means my hot water heater isn't working. I think I'll let Jason hose me down out in the yard, anyway. I wouldn't want to clog the drain with this ton of mountain I'm wearing.''

She stopped, waiting as he opened the door to the parking area outside, where Jason was waiting in the Blazer, the motor running. "Is he all right?" she asked, looking toward the vehicle.

"Jason?" Sean sighed. "I think so. We actually got along for nearly a minute, then I said something wrong and—hey, let's just get you home, all right?"

"Somebody should tell him that he hasn't been expelled," Cassandra said as she hobbled through the open doorway. "He's probably going out of his mind, waiting to hear."

"And he can wait a little longer," Sean said, feeling his jaw muscles tightening again. "I'll sketch in the basics once the two of us are home, and then let you fill in the blanks when he comes over to cut your lawn, or take out your garbage, or whatever the hell else you've got these kids doing."

She stopped so suddenly the crutch tips jammed against the sidewalk, nearly throwing her to the ground, and Sean with her. "You're so good at seeing everything with a sinister twist to it, aren't you, Mr. Frame?" she asked, her tone bitingly professional, crisp and unyielding. Nothing like the tone she had used earlier, when she had begged him—"Sean! Sean, *please!*"

But he couldn't help it. He had to say what was on his mind. "Do you really think it's ethical of you to have kids visiting you at home? Or is this how you think you can get them to achieve, to bend to your ideas of how they should behave? Are you intent on usurping *all* parental control over these kids? Where do parents fit in, Ms. Mercer—or don't they? Tell me, do I have a snowball's chance in hell with Jason as long as you're here, bandaging his wounds, cushioning his fall when he does something stupid, handing out sophomoric advice and freshly made cookies like some den mother—like some cult figure?''

''Cult figure! Did you hit your head when you fell, Mr. Frame? Because you're out of your tiny mind! No wonder Jason says you're a cross between Simon Legree and Attila the Hun! And I'll take a cab home, if you don't mind!''

''Hey, Ms. Mercer! Wow, neat crutches!''

Both Cassandra and Sean turned to see Jason unfolding his long legs from the truck, heading toward them.

Sean watched as Cassandra Mercer's features softened, smoothed, reassembled themselves into a smile he suddenly realized he would miss terribly if he never saw it again. ''Jason, you were wonderful,'' she told him, letting go of one crutch to touch his arm. ''You didn't panic, you didn't try to come looking for your father. You did precisely the right thing, notifying the authorities. I'm proud of you.''

Jason shot his father a look that said, *See? Not everyone thinks I'm stupid.* Then he said aloud, ''I didn't know you were stuck up there, too, Ms. Mercer. If I had, I would have gone over to see if Festus was all right. Boy, if he's still outside in this, he's going to be one mad cat!''

"That's true. He probably won't speak to me for a week. Or, until he hears me ripping off the top of his can of cat food." She looked past the Blazer, out over the quiet streets that glowed wetly in the late-morning hour. "Eerie, isn't it? You can forget how dark a rainy day can be, without the sun. No one expects the power to be restored much before tonight, or even Sunday morning. But I've also heard that the Sloane girl is alive, at least. They've located her. The news came in over the box from the ambulance crew that's out there, and one of the nurses told me."

"That's good news," Sean said, taking the clue from Cassandra and doing his best to act as if they were just three people having a normal conversation. Not two people who had just been intimate, extremely intimate, and the man-child who was both their concern and their shared problem.

Their shared problem? Sean repeated the thought, considered it. Was he out of his mind? Jason was his son, his problem—not Cassandra Mercer's! And he wasn't about to share his son with a woman with cockeyed ideas and theories. Not now, not ever! No way. No how. "Um…this mud is beginning to itch, Jason. Do you think we could get moving now?"

"Sure, Dad," Jason said, running to open the front passenger door of the four-door Blazer. "You can sit right here, next to me, Ms. Mercer," he said, then added with a grin, "I've spread an old blanket in the back seat, for the Mud Man."

"Thank you, Jason," Cassandra said, shooting Sean a triumphant look as she swung past him on the crutches, her purse hitting against her hip with each step she took. "I really do want to get home and take a long shower—hot or cold. I want to wash away all memory of the last eighteen hours, truly I do."

"If that was meant for me, Ms. Mercer," Sean said quietly as Jason went around to get in on the driver's side, "consider our feelings mutual."

And then he slammed her door shut and crawled into the back seat, aware that he looked like hell, that he probably smelled like a mud puddle, and that he had no intention—none whatsoever—of ever forgetting the very strange, very enlightening, very confusing night he and Cassandra had shared.

Seven

"Stop looking at me that way, darn it. Just stop! Or maybe you want me to buy bargain cat food again, huh? Believe me, I'm not above threats. Not today, anyway."

Festus Mercer, stray cat turned member of the family turned dictator for life, lifted his right front paw and began licking it. And he continued staring at Cassandra, who was sitting at the kitchen table, her wet hair in a towel, her body hidden beneath baggy royal blue sweats, and her eyes red from crying.

"I made a mistake, all right?" Cassandra continued as Festus opened his mouth impossibly wide, yawned, then stretched out on the braided rag rug on the floor in front of the sink.

"Okay. I made a *big* mistake. But it's not like I'm going to do it again or anything, you know. Unfortunately," she mumbled quietly, burying her chin against her closed fist as she rested her elbow on the table.

Taking a shower had been an ordeal. Not just because the water was nearly completely cold, but because she'd had to undress, remembering how Sean had undressed her. She had to soap up her body, remembering how Sean had run his hands over that body, molding her, shaping her, demonstrating to her that, in all of her almost twenty-eight years, she had never realized what it truly meant to be a female.

She had showered quickly, not because of the cold water, but because of the embarrassing heat of her body as she ran the soft net bath puff over her breasts, across her body. So aware. So aware.

Could she be pregnant?

"That's impossible!" she said out loud, so that the words might carry more weight, seem more legitimate.

But it wasn't impossible.

She had already checked her calendar, counting out the days since her last cycle, and knew that, biologically, she was somewhere near the tail end of her "fertile period," as Marie, one of her fellow teachers at Burke, had called it when she'd discussed her attempts at not only becoming pregnant but, this time, at conceiving a girl rather than another boy to join the two she already had at home.

So it *was* possible.

Just not "thinkable."

"So I won't *think* it," Cassandra said decisively, uncrossing her legs from beneath her and getting up from the chair as the teakettle began to whistle on the gas stove. She may not have heat, she may not have hot water or electricity, but she had her gas stove, thank God, and now she was going to have several hot cups of tea. Loaded with sugar. Creamy with milk.

"And topped off with at least six of the chocolate chip cookies I baked the other day," she told Festus, who looked up at her with a single eye, as if that was all he needed to see her clearly. "Want one?"

Festus sighed deeply, his rotund stomach rising and falling slowly, then closed his eye.

"Yeah, well, more for me, buddy," Cassandra said, then stopped with the cookie jar lid only partly raised. "Is this what I've come to? One-night stands and talking to dumb animals? God, I'll probably start crocheting doilies for toasters any day now. Then a cover for the microwave. And a blanket for the Jeep. Hey—think big, Cassandra. You can crochet a cozy that covers the whole damn house. You've got the time for it."

She lowered the lid on the cookie jar and sat back down in her chair. "I made love with the man," she said at last, staring at the clock on the wall, seeing that it had stopped at two minutes after seven—last night, Friday night, at two minutes after seven. "I made love with him, and he made love with me. A crazy impulse, a momentary pleasure, an aroused curiosity. Unprotected sex. Everything I warn the kids not to do, I did. And I did it with Sean Frame! *Twice!*"

That was what really got to her, she decided.

That she had made love with a man while trapped in a mud slide, possibly facing death—well, that was almost forgivable.

But for that man to have been Sean Frame, the man she had been fighting tooth and nail for two years? The man whose son she was counseling now, counseling and seeing as a criminally misunderstood kid whose father should be taken out and shot? The man whose long-lashed hazel eyes and clean, chiseled features had shown up in way too many of her maidenly dreams?

She buried her forehead in her hands. "Hanging's too good for me, Festus," she groaned, then jumped to her feet as someone knocked heavily on her back door. "Who...um...who is it?" she asked, her heart jammed so thoroughly in her throat that she could barely speak.

Please, please, don't let it be Sean Frame, here to check out my personal calendar!

"It's Jason, Ms. Mercer," she heard as she walked over to the door and pulled it open. "Hi! I thought you might need a couple of things, so I went shopping for you. Matt's with me, too, and Tammy and Becky. You don't mind that we're here, do you?"

Cassandra smiled and shook her head, stepping back a pace as the four teenagers trooped into her kitchen bearing milk, bread—and soda, two big bags of popcorn and the Monopoly board game. The milk and bread were nice touches, and undoubtedly sincere, but she knew the soda, popcorn and board game were the items that signaled a long, lazy Saturday of talk and laughter and relaxation.

"Head on into the living room, guys, and I'll be with you in a minute," she said as Jason opened her refrigerator and stuck the milk inside.

"That's going to go bad, isn't it, if the power doesn't come back on soon? No wonder they were giving it away at the supermarket," Jason said, shaking his head as if he'd just figured out a joke that had been played on him. "Are you okay? You look kind of like you aren't feeling so well, you know? Should we go away, let you sleep or something?"

"Sleep is the last thing on my mind, for some reason," Cassandra told him honestly. "I'm probably still too wired from our adventure last night, to tell you the truth. Jason—your father was wonderful up there. I think I would have been a screaming maniac if I'd had to have lived through it all without him."

Jason sniffed, then rubbed at the bottom of his nose with his knuckle as he turned his head away from Cassandra. "Yeah. That's Dad. The old brick in any crisis. Reliable. Dependable." He was grinding out the words, making them sound like character flaws. "Mature. Never does anything dumb. Nothing *criminal,* like his kid does."

"Jason, you are *not* a criminal!" Cassandra protested, putting her hand on his arm, wanting to reach out to him, wanting to hold him close, break down the brittle barriers he had put up around himself, around his heart. "I thought we'd talked some of this out? Did your father tell you the school board's decision? You haven't been suspended. You're on a sort of probation from now until school starts again in the fall. Released to my custody, as it were."

Jason put his head down, averting his eyes, allowing his long hair to fall forward, covering his face, saying nothing.

A knot of pain, of anger, formed deep in Cassandra's stomach. "Jason, he did *tell* you, didn't he?"

Eight

"Mr. Frame, there's a young woman out here who says she has to see you, but I've told her—"

"That I don't have an appointment. But I think I know the password—and maybe even the secret handshake. Do the words *horse's ass* ring any bells?" Cassandra Mercer said, brushing past Ms. Finley as she stood just inside the door to Sean's office, her hand on the knob, her body poised to act as blocker to any intruder who dared to enter her employer's inner sanctum without permission.

"Mr. Frame!" Ms. Finley exploded in her tight, exasperated way. "Shall I summon Security?"

Cassandra's long strides, made only marginally less impressive by her slight limp, ate up the half acre of beige Berber carpet between the door and the desk, and she leaned forward, flattening her palms on the custom-made rosewood surface. Her brown eyes flashed golden fire, her posture warned of her anger.

She was beautiful. Simply beautiful!

"Yes, Mr. Frame," she gritted out from between clenched teeth, "will you have her call Security? Have me tossed out on my ear?"

"It's all right, Ms. Finley, I know karate," Sean said as he pushed back his chair and stood up. The secretary reluctantly retreated, muttering unintelligibly.

Strange, he'd never realized what a humorless person his secretary was. Did she have to be so damn strict, so damn *earnest? Like you,* he thought about his own behavior, wincing. *Just like you.*

Once the door had closed on the woman's back, he spread his arms and smiled at Cassandra. "So nice to see that your ankle improved so much over the weekend."

"It hurts like hell, if you must know, but I can't take time to fool with both a taxi and those stupid crutches. Now—answer me, if you please. How could you have done that to Jason?"

"How could I have done what to Jason? What did I do to Jason? Oh, never mind. Whatever you think I did, or didn't do that I should have done, I plead guilty. And, obviously, hanging's too good for me. Now, do you want a cup of coffee?"

"What I *want,* Mr. Frame, is an explanation. How *dare* you not tell Jason about his probation?"

"Oh, so that's it." Sean decided he liked Cassandra's new "openness" with him, but not her temper. But at least she was no longer speaking to him in quotes from child guidance books.

He turned and walked to the rosewood sideboard and hefted the carafe holding a full Monday morning's supply of coffee. He kept his back to Cassandra, believing he was too angry to look at her directly, and concentrated on pouring two cups of the steaming brew. "You take yours heavy on both the sugar and the cream, I believe, if I remember correctly from our little visit to the hospital emergency room the other morning.''

''And you take yours black. Like your heart!''

Sean let out a short, exasperated chuckle, shaking his head. Okay, so maybe he did like her temper. Not that he was going to let *her* know that!

''You know, Cassandra, I never much cared for your controlled image at the board meetings, your prim body, your professional, uptight manner, your little voice quietly quoting ridiculous studies on teenagers in today's society, the values of interaction and positive reinforcement, yadda-yadda.''

''Yadda-*yadda?*''

He heard the amazement in her voice, and that made him relax even more.

''Yes. It's a technical term. But, to continue, it was a surprise, almost a pleasant surprise, to find out that you have another side to you, and a mouth and a brain that both seem to work independently of what you supposed to be the proper way to behave. But I think I'm ready to see you crawl back into your books and your cockeyed theories. In other words, Ms. Mercer, you're beginning to really get on my nerves.''

He picked up the two cups and walked back to the desk, sitting down once more and sipping at his coffee as he waited for her to pick up her own cup and either drink its contents or fling them in his face.

She was breathing through her nose, slowly, deeply, visibly trying to control herself. He watched as her hands, which had been drawn up into fists at her side, slowly flexed, her long fingers with their unpolished nails opening and closing as if she were debating whether or not she was strong enough to leap across the desk and strangle him.

And then she closed her eyes and let out a long breath in an audible sigh.

She was back in control of that unexpectedly wild, vibrant part of herself he had told her offended him but which, in fact, intrigued the hell out of him. The Secret Cassandra Mercer, the one she seemed to take out of hiding only when under considerable stress— or when she was dealing with Jason and her students. A more human Cassandra, with a biting wit, an open, sharing personality, and a sensual nature that had probably shocked her to her toes Friday night.

"Look, Mr. Frame. Sean," she began, running her hand over her tightly drawn-back hair as she collapsed into one of the chairs in front of the desk. "I'm not Jason's parent, I'm his guidance counselor. I am a part of his life for the next year, yes, but I am not trying to usurp your position in that life. He's yours to raise, to guide, to nurture. He's mine for six hours a day, five days a week. To talk to him, to listen to him. To try, some way, somehow, to *reach* him. To get him into a college you can brag about to your friends."

She lifted her hands from her lap. He watched them flutter in the air, as if she were trying to take hold of something that remained stubbornly beyond her reach, then settle in her lap once more. She was wearing another of those damned shapeless dresses that young women had taken to wearing—looking as sexless as pioneer women crossing the prairie to get to Colorado.

Why did women wear these things? Formless, the hems dragging just above their ankles, totally unappealing. Especially when he knew what was hidden beneath the blue-and-white-print cotton of Cassandra's dress. Wisps of lace, of satin. And a body whose sweet perfection had been burned into his mind.

Too late, too late, his mind chanted, although he'd never say the words aloud for fear she'd be destroyed, knowing he'd seen past her facade, knowing he remembered everything he'd seen with mind-blowing clarity. *I already know what you've been trying so damned hard to hide. I just don't know why.*

"Go on, Cassandra," he prompted when she didn't speak again. "I'm listening, honestly."

She shook her head. "No. No, you're not. Because if you were, if you'd understood a single word I've said in the past two years, in the few private meetings we've had about Jason since he came to Burke last year, you'd know that we're working at cross-purposes here, and have been from the beginning. You resent me, you resent my seeming interference in your raising of Jason, you resent that I know things about him that he's afraid to say to you—"

"Afraid?" Sean sat up straight in his chair and hit the intercom as it began to buzz. "Hold all my calls, Ms. Finley." He stood up and walked around the desk, to sit down beside Cassandra. "You're trying to tell me that Sean is *afraid* to talk to me? Now, that's a real joke! Obviously you haven't been around when he's told me, in no uncertain terms, where I can take myself, and precisely what I could do when I get there."

Cassandra laced her fingers together in front of her, leaning toward him. "No, no! I'm not saying you don't talk *at* each other—even yell at each other. You just don't talk *with* each other. You don't communicate. Like this business about his punishment for breaking the gym windows. Why didn't you tell him? Don't you know how frightened he's been, waiting for the ax to fall? He wants to play football next year, Sean, and he can't if he has to start off the new school year either suspended or on probation. That's why I fought so hard to make this arrangement where he earns money to pay off his debt, and does extra schoolwork this summer to show he's repentant."

Sean's brain had sort of floated away from Cassandra halfway through her explanation.

"He wants to play football?" he asked quietly, not caring that he was showing himself to be a near outsider in his own son's life. "I played football in high school and college. Quarterback. It's how I got my scholarship, how I got to college in the first place. Jason played some soccer back at his old school, but…he never said…I never knew…."

"He wants to try out to kick field goals, or something like that." Then she reached forward and laid a hand on his forearm. "Oh, Sean, I'm so sorry. He really doesn't talk to you, does he? I forgot that part."

She sat back in her chair again, sighing. "You know, I've read all these books, taken all these classes, and sometimes I wonder if it wouldn't be more effective to simply lock child and parents together in a padded room and not let them out until they *talk* to each other!"

Sean grinned. "As a school board member, I feel it my duty to point out that I seriously doubt our liability insurance covers that sort of thing." He stood up again, beginning to pace. "But, to get back to this probation thing. I'm imagining here that Jason went to your house on Saturday when he disappeared for hours, not saying where he was going?"

"You hate that, don't you?"

"That he went to your house?"

"No, that he didn't tell you he was coming over to my house." She shrugged. "Maybe both."

He scratched at his cheek, then rubbed his chin. "Yeah. I don't like it. After I finally got home and cleaned up, I fell into bed like one of the dead and only woke up slightly when I heard the door slam behind him as he was on his way out. I don't know. Maybe I should have told him right away, not waited. But I had a few other things on my mind. I told him when he finally wandered in sometime after eleven, walking right past the den and heading up the stairs without saying good-night."

"I'll bet you *yelled* the news at him," Cassandra said, shifting around in her chair, smiling up at him. Damn, she had a nice smile. Warm. Inviting. "I think I would have."

"It ended up being another of our rock-concert-decibel-intensity conversations, yes," he agreed, still looking at her, remembering that lush mouth, how it had felt, how it had tasted. "Cassandra," he began, then cleared his throat. "Have you thought any more about Friday night? About what I said concerning the possibility of—"

"I don't want to talk about that!" She leaped to her feet as if the chair had suddenly zapped her with an electric shock. "Seriously. Honestly. I just don't want to talk about that, think about that."

He put his hands on her shoulders, felt her trembling beneath his touch. "Well, that's too bad, Cassandra, because I do want to talk about it. And I can't stop thinking about it. About you. Please, can we have dinner tonight?"

Her eyes searched his face, nervously. Her expression telling him that she might want to put their interlude on the mountain behind her, but that she couldn't. A part of her, that part she had let him see Friday night, wouldn't let her. "I'm...that is, Jason is already..."

"Jason is coming to your house for dinner tonight?" Sean asked, thinking he knew what she was trying to say. That unexpected shaft of jealousy he'd felt before sliced through him again. "I don't believe this!" His fingers tightened around her shoulders.

"It's not what you think, Sean, for goodness sake!" Cassandra said, pulling away from him. "I've given Jason his first assignment, and he wants to go onto the Internet to do some research. I have a computer and modem at home, so it simply seemed easier to have him visit me. And have some dinner," she added quietly, wincing.

"I *am* guilty of interfering, aren't I?" she asked, obviously not wanting him to answer her. "I mean, he should be having dinner at home, with you. But he told me..." She closed her mouth with a nearly audible snap. "There I go again! I shouldn't tell you what Jason says, not unless I clear it with him first. This is getting entirely too involved, too difficult.''

"You don't have to say anything, Cassandra," Sean assured her. "I'm fairly certain I already know what Jason said. He said that his dad is working. His dad is always working. His dad doesn't give a flying flip what his son does, as long as his son doesn't cause him any trouble, get in his way. Right?"

She looked down at the carpet. "Well…"

"What he *didn't* tell you is that I have a pretty decent computer setup in my study at home. *And* an Internet connection."

Her head shot up, and he saw the Cassandra who had melted in his arms Friday night, who had turned to fire in his arms Friday night. "Why, that dirty little sneak!"

"My sentiments exactly," Sean said, smiling. "You said he's smart, and he is. Smart enough to play the two of us for chumps. Lying to you. Hiding his test scores, his love of football, from me. God knows what else he's doing! And I think it's time we called him on some of this, don't you?"

"You mean we might want to play 'guess who's coming to dinner?'"

"Exactly. When is he showing up at your door, to play his wounded-puppy act?"

"Six o'clock."

"I'll be there at six-thirty. I'll bring Chinese, if that's all right?"

"No. I've already got stew simmering in the slow cooker. It's Jason's favorite, and he asked me to make it for him."

"Save it for tomorrow night. It's time my son didn't get everything his own way, even if it's just a bowl of stew. We'll start with food and work our way up from there, okay? Are you in this with me, Cassandra? Neither of us can do it alone, you know."

She stood very still for a moment, then nodded. "You've got a deal." She picked up her purse—the damn thing looked like a feed bag, something else he obviously didn't understand about women's fashions—slung it over her shoulder and headed for the door.

"Oh," she said, turning back to him. "As long as we're joining forces here, I suppose I ought to tell you something. You remember what the other part of Jason's penance, for want of a better word, was?"

"You got him a part-time job to pay for the broken windows, right?"

"Yes, I did." Her smile told him she had done something daring, something more in line with the Cassandra he had met for the first time on Friday night, after knowing her for two years. "But, before I say anything, you have to promise not to let a word slip to Jason. Will you promise?"

"Cross my heart and hope to spit, if I remember that correctly from my checkered youth," Sean replied, and was rewarded with another of her spectacular smiles.

"All right. Just as long as you remember that you've promised, I suppose. He started his summer job this morning. Working on a loading dock. On *your* loading dock. I just thought you might want to know that. Now, remember—you promised!"

''Cassandra Mercer, you're an evil woman!'' Sean called after her as she practically ran out of his office.

And then he sat down behind his desk once more and laughed out loud. He laughed so long, and so hard, that Ms. Finley stuck her head into the office and asked if he was all right.

Which only made him laugh that much harder.

Nine

Cassandra sat on the couch in her living room, her feet tucked up beneath her, her eyes directed toward the television set, her mind a million miles away, occupied with thoughts of Sean Frame. The pain pill she had taken earlier was beginning to work on her sore ankle, which hadn't been helped by her foot-stomping explosion into his office that morning.

He had looked so good when she'd burst in on him. So controlled. So handsome. So much the successful businessman. So unlike the passionate, tousled man who had lain with her in the front seat of a Jeep poised to tumble off a mountain, grasping at life with both hands. Taking, giving, sharing.

Would she ever forget the feel of his mouth on her, his hands? They had been so intimate, more than simply casual lovers. They had clung to each other, knowing they might die, showing each other what it meant to be truly alive.

She would never have made it off that mountain alive without him. She might have tried to walk out with that man who had come stumbling by—the man who had reported sighting the Jeep, so that Jason's report of his father's disappearance was easily followed by their rescue.

The man had made it, of course, but that didn't mean she would have been as lucky. Why, she hadn't even been able to manage the twenty or so yards to the rescue truck without Sean's assistance! No, she would have slid right off that mountain if Sean hadn't convinced her that they were safer in the Jeep.

And, if she hadn't slid off the mountain, she probably would have gone stark, staring mad before the rescue team could find her. Alone. In the dark. Watching the storm explode around her. Watching the mountain dissolve above and below her. Sliding along that life-saving guardrail, metal screeching against metal, slamming into that boulder. Having the steering wheel slam into her.

Cassandra swallowed hard, feeling the fear rise up in her again, and deliberately focused on the news report now on the screen.

The tape they were showing looked vaguely familiar, and she sat forward, listening to the commentator speak about Randi Howell, renowned horsewoman, who had disappeared last Friday night, at the height of the storm.

"Now I remember!" Cassandra said to herself, picking up the remote control and raising the volume, listening closely as she watched the beautiful, blackhaired Randi put a gorgeous horse through its paces. She'd been at the horse show where Randi had performed so beautifully, captivating the crowd not only with her horsemanship but her winning smile and pure delight in what she was doing.

"She's disappeared?" Cassandra asked the commentator, who very politely answered her.

"Ms. Howell was last seen at the Squaw Creek Lodge shortly before seven last Friday night, where she was to have been wed to Hal Stuart, son of our late mayor, Olivia Stuart, who died that same evening. Her disappearance had been assumed to be a bride having second thoughts about the ceremony, but as Ms. Howell has not been seen since the lights went out at the lodge, and has not spoken with anyone in Grand Springs to confirm her reasons for disappearing, the police are investigating the case.

"Ms. Howell is five feet five inches tall, slim, with black hair and blue eyes. She was last seen—and we're not kidding here, folks—wearing a long white wedding gown and veil. Anyone with information about Ms. Howell's disappearance is to contact Chief Frank Sanderson at the Grand Springs Police Station."

"How far could she get in the dark, in the middle of a storm, wearing a wedding gown, for crying out loud?" Cassandra asked Festus, who was cleaning himself on the carpet in front of her. "I mean, she'd be a little *obvious,* right? Hard to hide in a crowd."

Visions of the Burt Reynolds, Sally Field movie, *Smokey and the Bandit,* flashed through Cassandra's mind, and she giggled, then just as quickly sobered. A woman in a wedding dress, alone in the dark in the middle of Friday night's storm might not be a good subject for a comedy. And that wedding dress wouldn't have stayed white for long if she'd been caught in one of the mud slides.

"I don't want to think about that," Cassandra declared flatly, hitting the button that turned off the TV set even as she stood and went to answer the doorbell. She was sure Jason was pressing on it as if the little button was the only thing holding him upright. Festus began to run in circles around the living room, unnerved by the sound.

"I'm coming, I'm coming, Jason!" she said, opening the door. "Festus is going to have your liver and lights if you don't stop doing that to him."

The teenager grinned and stepped inside the small foyer. "Gotta give the old guy some exercise. What are 'lights,' Ms. Mercer?" he asked, peeking in toward the living room where Festus was standing, his tail fat, his big yellow eyes narrowed as if contemplating leaping at Jason's head, then dragging his claws all the way down his body. Instead, the cat hopped up onto the couch, where he wasn't allowed to be, and lay down in the warm spot Cassandra had just left, which he wasn't allowed to do.

"I haven't the faintest idea, Jason," she told him, figuring it was useless to try to discipline Festus after the shock he'd had. She gestured that the boy should precede her down the hallway and into the kitchen. "I read it in a book, and it sounds fairly terrible, so I used it. Building my vocabulary, you know, one grossed-out expression at a time. Where's your notebook?"

Jason scratched behind his ear, looking sheepish. "I didn't bring one?" he said, making it into a question. "I should have brought one, shouldn't I?"

"As you're supposed to be taking notes, planning your first written report, yeah, I'd think you might need one. Never mind. I've got plenty of paper in my office. Do you remember how to sign-on to the Internet?''

Jason rolled his eyes as if she had just asked if he knew how to tie his sneakers—which it didn't look like he did, as his laces were always open. "You want the porno pages?" he asked, grinning. "I've never been, but I know how to get there. Build a bomb, see some really radical babes, find out the average yearly rainfall in Poughkeepsie.... You name it, I can find it for you on the Internet.''

"I'd rather you stuck to researching the history of glass, if you don't mind," she said, putting her hands on his shoulders, turning him around and pointing him in the general direction of the small office behind the kitchen. "The report is due this Friday, remember? But first, how was work?''

Jason pulled out a chair and sat down at the kitchen table, his hazel eyes, so like his father's, suddenly alive with excitement.

"You wouldn't believe it!" he began as she went to the refrigerator and pulled out two cans of soda, popping the tops and handing one to him before she leaned against the counter, giving him her full attention. "They've got this system, see, for inventorying everything as it comes in off the trucks. All computerized. What it is, where it goes, that sort of thing. Same thing for stuff going out. And it's a mess, Ms. Mercer! A *joke!* I mean, whoever designed that software has to be a total jerk!''

Cassandra shook her head, taking a deep breath, remembering the break-in of their school computer system last December, and the ''Kilroy was here—

and me, too!'' that was left behind, showing that the teacher's grades folders had been opened without authorization. Nothing had been destroyed, nothing had been altered, but they had all known that it could have been, if the hacker had wanted to make a mess.

Nobody had ever been caught, although she had been fairly certain she'd seen Jason Frame's ''fingerprints'' all over the incident. After all, he was smart. And smart included knowing the World War II graffiti slogan about Kilroy.

''This is just a sort of an off-the-wall question, Jason. Humor me, won't you? How well do you know your William Faulkner?'' she asked now, looking at him with eyelids narrowed.

His grin was beyond devilish as he quoted, '' 'Really, the writer doesn't want success.... He knows he has a short span of life, that the day will come when he must pass through the wall of oblivion, and he wants to leave a scratch on that wall—Kilroy was here—that somebody a hundred, or a thousand years later will see.' That the quote you're talking about, Ms. Mercer? I'll bet it is.''

''Difficult to believe you had a D in literature last semester. And only a C in your Basic Computer class. Jason,'' she said carefully, tilting her head to look at him closely, ''you didn't *do* anything with your father's computer system, did you? Please, tell me you didn't do anything. I mean, it was your *first* day!''

He took a long drink of soda, his head thrown back so that she could watch his Adam's apple moving up and down as he chug-a-lugged the cold liquid. ''It's all right, Ms. Mercer,'' he said after he'd put down the can and wiped a hand across his grinning mouth. "Herb said I should give it a shot after I dazzled him with a few terms and showed him how I'd reconfigure the flowchart so it was easier to read. Herb's about fifty-five or so, and he can't get used to his new bi-focals."

Sean's going to kill me. Kill me dead. Have my liver and lights. Well, at least then maybe I'll find out what lights are.

Cassandra sighed, her eyes closed, then groaned theatrically. "Oh, Jason, how could you? You were just supposed to show up, lift a few boxes, make a few dollars, learn the meaning of hard work, then pay for the damage you did at the school."

She opened her eyes again, glaring at him. "But not you. Oh, no. Not Jason Frame. *You've* got to show up, reprogram an entire computer system. Does it work?"

His grin lit up the entire kitchen. "Did you ever doubt it?" he asked, openly proud of himself. "Herb called his boss, who listened to my suggestions, tried them out—and I've been promoted. Gotta wear a tie to work tomorrow, as a matter-of-fact. And I'm on salary now. And enrolled in the management training program Dad set up for gifted teens, or something like that. And all on my own merit, too! It was a stroke of genius, Ms. Mercer, signing me up as Jason Taylor. Dad doesn't even know I'm there!"

"Wanna bet?" Cassandra mumbled under her breath, beginning to see herself as a tennis ball, being batted back and forth by the two Frame men.

Louder, she said, "Just remember that you still

have another year of high school, young man. You can't go climbing the corporate ladder until you're out of college. Which,'' she continued pointedly, ''you can't go to unless you graduate from high school, which won't happen unless you get yourself into that office and start researching the history of glass. Right?''

''Right,'' Jason agreed, unfolding his length from the chair, then turning back to pick up the soda can before heading to the office. He stopped at the door and sniffed the air. ''Funny, I don't smell anything cooking. Where's the stew?''

''I decided on Chinese, instead,'' Cassandra said, just wishing Jason would go to the office, turn up the CD player and become his usual oblivious self before his father arrived. ''We'll have stew another time, all right?''

Jason shrugged. ''No problem. Call me when it comes, okay, and I'll help you set everything up?''

Cassandra gripped the countertop with both hands as she leaned her back against it, her knees buckling. ''No problem. Right, Jason.''

Then she added, in a barely audible whisper, ''Oh—and did I tell you that your Dad is joining us?'' He didn't hear her, of course. She couldn't even hear herself over the nervous sound of the loud pounding of her heart.

Sean looked at the long green-and-white printout as Herb Larkin explained the changes that had been made, nodding at all the right times, asking all the right questions. ''So what you're saying, Herb, is that this new configuration removes two of the steps from our former checklist, yet increases our inventory accuracy by—what was that, twenty-three percent?''

"Yes, sir," Herb answered, bobbing his head excitedly. "That's how Jerry figures it. The more steps you take, the more chances of human error, or something like that. And this kid—this *kid*—he just looked at the program for about an hour. I had him sitting near me to watch, it being his first day on the job and all, and he's watching me, watching me, and I'm logging in stuff and logging out stuff and making all the checks, and I'm moaning and groaning over all the different screens I have to pull up, all the different checks and balances before I'm cleared to move on to the next stuff, and he says, hey, that's dumb! Why don't you just…well, I guess I already told you that part before, huh, Mr. Frame?"

"Yes, Herb. Yes, you did." Sean paged through the printout a third time, still comparing it with the one that had been put on his desk Friday night—he had a printout from the loading dock placed on his desk every night—and shook his head. "It was right there, right in front of me. And I'm the one with the master's degree in computer science. Damn."

"Of course, we didn't let the kid do any of the actual changes. I mean, hey, he's a kid, right? But I took him to Jerry, and they talked it all out, and then they did the work between them. I don't know what they did. These computers are Greek to me, you know. And now Jerry took the kid from me and put him in with him."

"Jerry did that, did he?" Sean looked at the two

printouts again, then sat back in his desk chair. "And this boy's name would be?" he asked, somehow already sure of the answer Herb would give him.

"Jason," Herb said, still nodding. Herb nodded a lot, as if he was always in agreement with himself. "Jason Taylor."

Sean's smile disappeared. "Taylor?" He sat forward once more, punching a few keys on his own computer, tapping into the personnel files. And there it was: Jason Taylor. He hadn't used his own name, but his mother's new married name. The boss's son, the owner's son, and he hadn't used his own name. Herb hadn't indulged the kid, Jerry hadn't been trying to score points. The kid had come up with a good idea. A damn good idea. And all on his own.

Was this the same kid who couldn't find a clothes hamper if it were the size of a compact car and parked in the middle of his bedroom?

"Well, thanks, Herb," Sean said, reaching out to shake the man's hand. "We'll watch this, see how it goes. There could be a few glitches that haven't shown up after only one day. You'll keep me informed?"

"Yes, sir," Herb said emphatically, then added, "you know, sir, these kids today are something else. I mean, this Taylor boy shows up this morning, long hair, ripped jeans, T-shirt with some dead rock star on it, a flannel shirt six sizes too big hanging over it—looking like he can't remember his own name, you know. And then he does something like *this!*" He pointed to the spreadsheets. "I don't get it. Why do they do this?"

"Do what, Herb?" Sean asked, knowing exactly what his son had looked like before leaving the house this morning because he had watched out the window, from behind the bedroom curtains, believing the boy had deliberately dressed like a homeless orphan to embarrass his father.

"I don't know, sir—*hide?* Yeah, that's it. They hide. Like they don't want anyone to notice them, ask anything of them, *expect* anything from them. You'd think their parents would grab hold of them, tie them down, cut off all that hair, give them a bath and make them wear decent clothes."

"You're not married, are you, Herb?" Sean asked, not angry but more amused by Herb's idea of cleaning up a teenager's act. "No wife, no kids?"

"No, sir," Herb said, nodding once more. "No wife, no kids. I've got six older brothers, and more than two dozen nieces and nephews. I've seen plenty, let me tell you. And I never saw the point in all that hassle of raising a bunch of ungrateful kids, to tell you the truth."

Sean picked up the printouts again, smiling. "Oh, I don't know, Herb. Parenthood has its rewards. Really, it's got its rewards."

"If you say so, sir. Well, I'd best be punching out. It's almost six-thirty."

Sean pushed back his sleeve and looked at his watch. Where had the time gone? Damn it! This was what Sean was always complaining about—how his father always had time for business but never enough time for him. Not that Jason knew they were meeting at Cassandra's tonight.

"I'll walk out with you, Herb," he said, picking up the suit jacket that had been draped over the back of his chair. He could call the Chinese takeout from his car phone, pick up the order at the drive-through and be at Cassandra's house in twenty minutes. Tops.

And then what? he asked himself as he turned to his left in the employee parking lot, heading for his newly repaired Mercedes. *Yeah, Frame. Then what? You're ordering Chinese food, not a serving of crow.*

Ten

Melissa Etheridge was belting out another chorus of "Bring Me Some Water," and Cassandra danced around the kitchen, caught up in the pulsing beat of the music. Jason had cranked the stereo to the "ouch" level, and the bass was thumping in her chest, the drumbeat in the background causing her to bob her head with the rhythm, her bottom lip caught between her teeth, the music singing in her blood.

She picked up the long-handled, plastic pot scrubber and used it like a microphone, growling the words into it as she shook her head, shook her shoulders, allowed herself to be moved by the beat, set free by the beat. She swung around in a circle, the pot scrubber turning into a guitar as she "air-played" the riff, felt her unbound hair slap against her cheeks.

She pushed in Jason's chair with a flip of her hip, picking up the empty soda can and winging it into the recycling container before pulling the pot scrubber to her mouth, and complaining that she was "burning alive!"

The singer broke into the hard, thumping refrain once more, and Cassandra shifted into high gear—her hips swaying, her feet slip-sliding along the smooth tile as she opened the refrigerator, pulled out another can of soda, made her way to the office door, pulled it open and danced her way inside.

Jason looked over his shoulder, saw her and grinned as he came to his feet. He immediately turned up the stereo another notch, took the soda away from her, then leaned in close as the song blared to its heart-thumping crescendo—at which time, their knees bent, their heads pressed together, they sang the last line together.

Jason put his arm around Cassandra, to keep her from tumbling to the floor, and the two of them laughed at each other as the rock star began singing another song.

And then he looked toward the kitchen, and his expression turned hard. His eyes went flat and dull, and his lip curled. "What's *he* doing here?" he asked, wheeling away from Cassandra, who had been laughing and trying to catch her breath.

"Curses. Foiled again," Cassandra muttered even as she stood up straight, pushed the hair out of her eyes and turned to look at Sean Frame.

She was more than a little aware of her closely fitting striped knit top and her cutoff jeans—hadn't she been on her way upstairs to change? She had a vague memory of thinking it was time to head for the stairs, right before Jason had put on the Etheridge CD. She crossed her hands over her waist and said as cheerily as she could, "Oh, didn't I tell you your dad was coming to dinner? Gee. I must have forgotten."

"You also forgot to lock your front door," Sean pointed out as he walked into the office, which suddenly seemed much too small to hold the three of them. "I put the box of food on the kitchen table, then followed the noise. You two planning to take that act on the road?"

Jason sniffed. "Yeah. Right, Dad. Ha. Ha. Look, Ms. Mercer, I can't stay."

He brushed past Cassandra, on his way to the door, but she grabbed his arm, stopping him. "Jason, don't go. I know I should have told you that your father was coming over. He—he wanted to say thank you for Friday night."

Sean's voice was pure black velvet and held more than a hint of teasing. "Yes, indeed, Cassandra. I certainly do."

Her eyes wide, she shot him a shocked look. "I mean, that is—for picking him up." As Sean's smile, which had appeared when she'd made her first foot-in-mouth statement, widened appreciatively, she went on quickly, "No. I didn't pick him up. Well, not exactly. I mean, I *did* pick him up. Well, at least *technically*. But I...Jason, can you please turn down the stereo?"

Jason did as she'd asked, and the silence in the office instantly became deafening.

"Yeah, well, I guess you two want to be alone. And, like I said, I gotta go now," Jason muttered as he shut down the computer and began picking up the pages he had printed out.

"Jason, don't be an idiot," Sean said as his son brushed past him, which really helped matters a *whole* lot, in Cassandra's opinion. Not!

"Jason," she said, following him into the kitchen. "Your dad didn't mean that the way it sounded. He brought dinner for the three of us, so let's all just sit down and eat, okay? Can't we do that?''

Sean followed them into the kitchen, then leaned up against the counter, watching his son, watching Cassandra. At least he wasn't saying anything anymore, thank goodness. Because that sort of ''help'' she didn't need!

Jason looked at his dad again. ''No. I don't think so.'' He shook his head, his jaw twisted as his eyes narrowed, in anger, in pain. ''You just had to horn in, didn't you. You couldn't leave well enough alone, leave *me* alone. Not even this once! I can't have anything to myself, can I, Dad? Not anything...or anybody. Aw, hell, I'm outta here!''

And then he was gone, the front door slamming behind him, and Cassandra and Sean were alone together in the kitchen, a big cardboard box full of fried rice and spare ribs filling the air with heady aromas—which did nothing to block out the smell of tension, of disquiet, of hot, juvenile anger.

''I—I was just on my way upstairs. To change,'' Cassandra explained, wishing she hadn't had to witness such an embarrassing, painful family moment.

''No need, Cassandra. I've seen you dressed less *professionally* than this,'' Sean told her as he slipped out of his suit jacket and undid his tie. ''You won't mind if I get comfortable, will you?''

''Look, I know you're angry and all that, but calling him an idiot was nasty, Sean, and beneath you.'' She spread her arms helplessly, then clasped her hands together. ''I—I...oh, damn it! Why didn't I warn him? That poor kid! Shouldn't you be going after him?''

Sean pulled out a chair and sat down, reaching into the cardboard box. ''No, Cassandra, I shouldn't. And neither should you, just in case you were thinking about it. He's made his statement and I think we both understand the why of it. He thinks I'm cutting in on his girl. Now, as I haven't had lunch today and most of this stuff turns into unrecognizable goo when it gets cold, let's eat.''

Sean ate, but every bite was an effort. Cassandra didn't even bother pretending to do more than push food around on her plate. They sat across from each other in silence, Jason's parting words hanging between them: ''I can't have anything to myself, can I, Dad? Not anything…or anybody.''

Finally, Sean gave up even the pretense of eating and laid down his fork. ''I wasn't just saying that to be mean, you know. He's got a crush on you. And, from the looks of it, a pretty big one.''

Cassandra nodded, keeping her head down, then looked up at him, her eyes filled with tears. ''I had no idea. None. I should have. I should have known, right from the beginning. But I didn't. I didn't see it, didn't think it. All the kids come over here. They always have. We play Monopoly, they help me with yard work, I cook them hamburgers and hot dogs on the grill. They shovel me out in the winter. It's always been like that, from the beginning.''

''From the beginning? How long has this been going on?''

"Since a few months after I started at Burke, I guess. I—I just feel comfortable with these kids, you know, and they feel comfortable with me. Then we talk colleges and careers and SAT scores—and they don't even know they're learning anything until they come to me, sometimes months later, and say, 'Hey, Ms. Mercer—I've decided on my major, I'm going to study biology.' Or computer math, or library science…'' Her voice broke, trailed off.

"And you never thought you were getting a little too close?" Sean asked, gathering up the small white boxes and shoving them all back into the cardboard carton.

She shook her head. "Most of the ones who come here are the only child in their family, like I was. It isn't really *me* they're coming to visit, but one another. And they're all good kids. Really good kids. They just sort of hang out here, you understand, and I act as chaperone. They come here during the school year and hold study groups, work on class projects together. I grew up in a quiet house. A neat, tidy, never-raise-your-voice-or-the-volume-on-the-stereo kind of house. It's not much fun."

"But they have fun when they come here, right?" Sean pushed on, watching Cassandra closely, believing he was beginning to understand a lot more about her than he had before this evening. "And you have a family."

She wiped quickly at her eyes, stood up and turned away from him. "Something like that," she admitted. "But I never imagined that…"

"That my son would develop a mansize crush on

you?'' Sean put in helpfully as she took a deep breath, then let it out slowly. This wasn't at all easy for her, for either of them.

"Yes. That,'' she answered quietly. She kept her back to him. "I should never have allowed my association with the kids go beyond the guidance office, no matter how well it was working out. It was unprofessional. Stupid. If you want my resignation, you'll have it in the morning. I know you want to leave now. Thanks for the dinner. I can clean it up myself.''

Sean had no intention of leaving, never had. He stood up and walked around the table. Standing behind her, he put his hands on her shoulders, beginning to rub them, take some of the obvious tension out of her muscles. "I don't want your resignation, Cassandra. And I know you meant well when you started inviting the kids here.''

She leaned her head forward, so that his thumbs could work at the tense muscles in her neck. "I never actually invited anyone. They just started showing up.''

"I see.'' Sean felt the heat of her body under his hands, tried not to think about it. "Like Topsy—it all just growed, huh?''

She nodded. "Kind of like that, yes. First a few of the girls, then the boys started coming. All the outsiders, the computer nerds, the loners. And then, a couple of months ago, Jason started coming, as well. And now they're a group. Even as some of them graduated and went off to college last year, new, younger kids started showing up to take their place. They found an identity with one another, I think you could call it, a common bond. Their parents know they come here. I've talked to many of them at school, or on the phone when they call to remind their kids to come home for supper. You're the only one who never called, but Jason swore you knew he was coming here.''

She pulled away, turned to look up at him. In her bare feet, without the high heels she usually wore, she looked so much smaller to him, so feminine, so fragile. ''Your son is a smooth talker, Sean, if you don't already know that. I think he could make people believe the Rocky Mountains are made of Silly Putty.''

Sean took her hand and led her into the living room, waiting until she dislodged a huge, fairly ugly cat he was sure was Festus—because he definitely looked like a Festus—from the couch and sat down beside her. ''Look, Cassandra,'' he began, wondering what he would say, what he *could* say, ''I'm not here to pass judgment on your methods, although you probably couldn't tell that from the run-ins we've had at board meetings the past two years.''

''You're right,'' she said, smiling softly, leading him to believe she was slowly regaining her composure, ''I couldn't. But, please, don't let that stop you. You were saying?''

He laughed, shaking his head. ''I'm off balance here, Cassandra, do you know that? For two years, you've been the enemy. Not only the enemy, but a whole other Cassandra Mercer. Uptight, professional, downright bossy at times. So sure of yourself and your theories.''

"I tried to be professional," she explained quietly, her proud chin tipping a little, showing her underlying temper, the one he'd never supposed existed when she was being cool and polished and oh-so dignified as she spoke at board meetings.

"And you had the role down pat, for two whole years. Then, last Friday night, I met a new Cassandra Mercer. One with a temper, a sense of humor and a fairly wicked tongue. A woman with fire and passion and—if I can say this without your taking a swipe at me?—some of the sexiest damn underwear in history. And now look at you—your hair down, dressed in cutoff jeans? I know from your personnel file that you're twenty-seven, but right now you don't look much older than Jason. Who are you, Cassandra? Who are you, really?"

She shook her head, then pushed a hand through her hair, so that the golden brown strands moved away from her face, then fell in a sleek curtain, obscuring her profile. "I'm one of the loners, Sean," she said at last, turning to smile at him. "Only child, misfit, too brainy for my own good. And very, very good. Miss Goody-Two-Shoes, right down to the straight-A grades and being the only girl in the senior class who wasn't invited to the prom. Your typical outsider, that was me. Telling myself it didn't matter, that being popular wasn't all it was cracked up to be—then spending my Saturday nights at home, helping my mother correct term papers. I look at these kids, and, well, I guess that saying that's going around sums it all up. You know it—been there, done that, got the T-shirt."

"I was the captain of the football team," Sean told her, which he knew said a lot more than the few words he'd spoken.

She grinned at him. "Ah, yes! I know the type. You were one of *them,* weren't you? Cheerleaders following you around. Had your own little clique, which, of course, was the *in* crowd. Hanging out together after school, riding around town on Saturday nights, scoping out the girls. Drinking with your buddies under the bleachers. So, were you king of the prom?"

"Yeah," Sean said shortly, wincing, and considering going home and burning his high school yearbooks. All of them featured one Sean Frame prominently—photographs of him as class president, football captain, as well as a member of the Honor Society. Jason didn't appear in any of his undergraduate yearbooks except in the obligatory junior class picture.

He grinned sheepishly, guiltily. "I was also one of the guys who made fun of the misfits. I may have been an orphan, but I attacked high school, and college, like they were mountains to be climbed, both academically and socially. I wanted to fit in, and I made damn sure I did, no matter what it took, no matter that I left school at three to go back to a foster home or the children's shelter. People thought I was noble. I wasn't, Cassandra. I was ambitious, and fairly ruthless. And a real first-class jerk, now that I look back on it all—now that I'm mature enough to stand back and look at the reasons Sally and I ended up in the back of the '68 Chevy."

"Have you ever told Jason any of this? It might help him, you know, learning about your background, your struggle."

Sean shook his head. "He doesn't know anything about my childhood—or his own, if you want to get technical about it. I wanted to protect him, protect his mother. No, that's not true. I wanted to protect myself."

"You two really have to have a talk. Maybe all three of you should have a talk. A whopping great *bunch* of talks!" Cassandra's smile was sweet, and knowing, and decidedly unsettling. "Jason told me his dad is Mr. Perfect. I don't think it was a compliment, frankly. Did you ever consider that Jason might be trying his best *not* to be like you, or what he perceives to be the real you?"

"Are you saying that Jason deliberately set out to be one of the misfits?"

She laid a hand on his arm. "Oh, no, no! *None* of them are misfits! There *are* no misfits, you see. There are only *kids*. Some of them just have a more difficult time growing up, that's all. A harder time fitting in, because they're already individuals, unwilling or unable to be part of the herd. And they'll be fine, just fine, once they go to college, get out in the real world. It's just that a teenager's world is so small, that the *different* ones, well, they sort of stick out more, you know?"

"Jason doesn't exactly fade into the background, I'll give him that," Sean said, considering everything Cassandra had said, considering what she *hadn't* said. Jason felt it was impossible to live up to his father's achievements, so he was doing his best to make his own mark, his own way. Was that it? Was that what his son was doing? "There are times, like when I visit the school for assemblies, and see the whole study body in the auditorium, then spy Jason, that I think he sticks out like a sore thumb."

"I know. If you're not an athlete, or very pretty…if your skin is more like the 'before' than the 'after' photo in the acne cream ads…if you understand physics while the rest of the kids are still stuck on fractions…if you're honest enough to admit that you actually *liked* reading Shakespeare… Well, for those kids, high school can sometimes be worse than a four-year trip to hell."

Sean scratched his cheek. "And you're saying that Jason is one of the *individuals*—isn't that what you called them? So why the lousy grades? Why the broken windows in the gym?"

Cassandra stood up and began to pace, obviously unaware of what the sight of her long, straight legs was doing to Sean's concentration. "I believe Jason was trying to fit in, and hunting for a new way to do it. He's always been trying to fit in, find a niche somewhere, find an identity. Good grades didn't do it at his old school, so he started cutting class when he transferred to Burke, acting up in class, deliberately not doing well on his tests. We both know his grades were good, even exceptional, until he transferred here for his junior year."

"His grades were excellent. I thought he was failing his courses to punish me for taking him away from his mother, although he said he'd wanted to go.

It never occurred to me that he was afraid of being unpopular, that he'd ever *been* unpopular.''

"I think he felt he'd be more accepted if he hid his talents, his brains, so he set about becoming a rebel, and it came back to bite him. Which is why he changed his tactics lately, going out for football, allowing the group that comes here to see his intelligence, his promise, his real personality. As for the rest of it, the clothes, the haircut, the belligerence—well, I believe that to be nothing more than a cry for your attention, although I still find it difficult to believe he broke those windows.''

Sean felt the muscles in his jaw begin to tighten. "*Whose* attention?''

She stopped pacing and bent down to pick up Festus, who had been threading himself between her legs, meowing. She held the cat's enormous belly against her face, rubbing her cheek against its fur.

"*Your* attention, Sean,'' she said quietly. "Yours, your ex-wife's. And, yes, maybe a little of mine, now that I think about it, now that I look back on the way he behaved once he heard about the group that comes here, and why they come here. But mostly your attention, I believe.''

Sean felt sick to his stomach. No wonder he hadn't wanted to listen to Cassandra's theories, her explanations. They hurt too much. "Well, he's damn well got it, I'll give him that,'' he said bitterly. "But why this way?''

"I guess I'd have to be a seventeen-year-old boy to answer that one,'' Cassandra said, still standing in the middle of the room, still keeping her distance. "At least he didn't decide to experiment with drugs, or slit his wrists, like one of the girls did last year when her parents separated and her best friend moved to Vail. That was a tough one, but she's fine now, doing well in school, coming over here with the rest of the gang.''

She sighed, allowing Festus to hop down to the carpet, for he was beginning to squirm in her arms. "I wouldn't be a teenager again for anything. They're all so young, so vulnerable, so very confused.''

Sean sat back against the couch, his legs spread out in front of him. "That's a hell of a thing, Cassandra— to feel grateful that Jason didn't try to kill himself. Jason is my son? God, I feel like I'm living with a stranger!''

Cassandra returned to the couch, sitting down beside him once more. She no longer looked quite so young, although she was still the most beautiful, the most desirable woman he'd ever seen. And probably one of the most intelligent. "How did you get past the misfit stage, Cassandra?'' he asked, then instantly wished back the words as her golden brown eyes darkened.

"By flunking out of two colleges,'' she said shortly, her smile wan. "Did I mention that my parents were both college professors? Dad had a heart attack when I was put on academic probation at the third college they shoved me into—and that's when I finally woke up. I woke up to a lot of things, a lot of old problems and the new problems I had made in trying to forget them. You see, *they* were never going to change, my parents were never going to see me as anything but their product, the melding of their exceptional genes. And, at that time, as their greatest disappointment. I so wanted them to see me for who I really was, or who I thought I really was. Except that I didn't know who that could be—I just knew I wasn't happy being Cassandra Mercer, daughter of. Cassandra Mercer, superbrain. Cassandra Mercer, plain Jane nerd.''

She laughed softly. ''Not that I could change my outside all that much. I'm still the professors' daughter, even with the both of them dead these past five years. Why, I had to fight down the impulse to wear white gloves to my first employment interview. I still wear my glasses most of the time, although I only need them to drive, and I have a pair of contact lenses around here somewhere. I'm still a whole bunch of different Cassandras, trying to make up one livable whole.

''But there are times—'' she hesitated, squeezing her hands into fists as if trying to hold on to something too fleeting to be captured ''—times when I begin to feel that newer, more complete Cassandra Mercer I'm searching for blossoming inside me, begging to be let out.''

She turned to him, her eyes bright with tears. ''I think…I think I'm having the best of my high school days right now, at twenty-seven. Through these kids, these wonderful, confused, beautiful kids, I'm catching up on all that I missed, helping them to find all that they shouldn't be forced to miss just because they're looked upon as *different*.''

She shook her head, sighed. "I don't know. Maybe I'm the one who needs guidance counseling."

Sean sat quietly, remembering Friday night, remembering how it felt to hold Cassandra in his arms, make love to her. "Last Friday…" he began slowly, hunting for the right words, sure he was going to find all the wrong ones. "You were a virgin, Cassandra. I thought, at the time, that we were giving in to the impulse of the moment. That, and reacting to the distinct possibility that we might not make it off that road alive. But it was more than that for you, wasn't it? I was the high school jock, and you were the cheerleader, making out in a parked car while the windows steamed up around us. That's what I was. Another *experience* you missed in high school, in college. Wasn't I?"

She sat very still, searching his face with her steady gaze. "I don't know," she said at last, her honesty ripping at his gut. "I only know it was a mistake."

He took refuge in anger. "Oh, yeah, lady, it was that, all right," he said, standing up, looking down at her and wishing she didn't look so vulnerable, so damned irresistible. "I guess we can only hope that when the kids come over to play, you're mixing a few lectures on safe sex in with your Monopoly games and gardening and dirty dancing."

"That was uncalled-for, and you know it," Cassandra said as she, too, stood up.

"Yeah?" Sean shot back, knowing he was being more immature than his son had been at the age of three—and definitely feeling much more highly sexed than he himself had been when he was spending time in cars parked on the side of the road after midnight. "If you think that was uncalled-for, what do you think of this?"

Before she could react, before he could tell himself to be rational, he grabbed her shoulders, pulled her tightly against him and crushed his mouth down on hers. He ground his lips against her, forced his thigh between hers, slid his hands down her back to cup her buttocks, pressed their bodies together.

His was a blatant sensual assault, meant to let her know that he was more than an experience, an experiment.

Because he was a man.

Because he was the man who had made love to her. The man she had begged to "please, please, don't stop" only a few nights ago.

The man who had been torturing himself with dreams of her ever since then.

Just as he was mentally badgering himself back to some semblance of sanity, Cassandra slid her arms around his back, her fingernails digging into his skin, her pelvis tipping upward, straining against him. Her mouth opened, allowing him entry, and her tongue dueled with his, daring him, urging him on.

He dragged his mouth away from hers, pressing her head against his shoulder as his lips moved along her cheek, against her throat. He took her earlobe into his mouth, bit it softly—just as she was biting at his neck, running her tongue along the top of his opened shirt collar.

The heat they had generated inside the stranded Jeep was back, tenfold. The passion, the longing, the wanting. No shy virgin now, she was giving as good as she was getting. And he wanted to give her more, take more.

"I know who you are, Cassandra Mercer," Sean breathed into Cassandra's ear, holding her close even as she moved in his arms, belatedly trying to escape him. "You're heat, and fire, and passion. And I've been burned, Cassandra. I'm still burning. I'm no teenager, and neither are you. You want me and, God help me, I want you. I want you here and now, and the only thing keeping me from carrying you upstairs is the fact that I'm still as unprepared for you as I was Friday night. Our child could already be growing inside you. But you want to know something, Cassandra? Do you want to know what I'm thinking? If there is no child of mine inside you now, then there damn well should be."

The sound of the front door slamming shut, rattling the glass panes, tore them apart. Cassandra ran to the window. "Oh, my God. It was Jason! He came back, probably to apologize to us." She turned to Sean, her expression stricken. "He *saw* us! He probably *heard* us! What are we going to do?"

Sean smacked his closed fist against his forehead, calling himself the worst sort of fool. "I'll go after him," he said, turning for the kitchen, where he had left his suit jacket and keys.

"No, don't do that. Not now, while he's so angry," Cassandra said, following after him, tucking her knit shirt back into her waistband. He didn't even remember having pulled it free, although he did remember sliding his fingers along her spine, across her rib cage, cupping her breast, tugging down her bra....

He picked up his jacket and turned back to her, anger burning inside him. Anger at himself. At her. "Look, Jason is still my son. I think I know how to handle him."

He brushed past her, out onto the front porch and stopped dead. Jason was nowhere in sight. Which was probably a good thing, because Sean realized he *didn't* know how to handle his son, didn't have the faintest idea what he would say to the boy if and when he found him.

Eleven

Cassandra wasted several sleepless hours tossing and turning until nearly four in the morning before giving up and going downstairs to pour herself a glass of milk in hopes that it would help settle her still nervous stomach.

She stopped at the doorway to the kitchen, seeing a dim glow of light under the office door, and decided that Jason must have turned on a lamp while he was working and she had forgotten it when she'd checked the house before going up to bed.

She had forgotten the light, but she couldn't forget what had happened in her lonely, quiet house earlier that evening. The shambles she had made out of her life, and possibly out of Jason's, who was the innocent victim of her stupidity, her reckless passion, her unhappy, unfulfilled youth.

She put her hand on the refrigerator handle, then hesitated. Milk had been her mother's answer to a sleepless night, a stomachache, to any sort of trouble. It had never been Cassandra's.

"It should have been," she mumbled, pulling on the handle and blinking against the light that came on inside the refrigerator. She looked at the milk carton, pulled a face and lifted out a can of soda instead, popping the top as she went over to the table and sat down.

Surely she'd had worse nights. Longer nights. More traumatic nights.

But never a more lonely night.

She'd been avoiding thinking about the whys and wherefores of her actions of last Friday night. As self-protection, in self-defense. Because she knew she wouldn't like the answers she'd find behind the reasons.

Curiosity. Fear. Impulsiveness. Fear. Attraction. Fear. Fascination. Fear. Desire. Fear.

Love?

How easy it would be, how soothing to her tortured mind, if she could say, "Well, I was in love with the guy. It was one of those classic love-hate attractions, you know. Always there, for the past two years. This undercurrent between us, this silent, physical connection, this cosmic attraction. A certain heat, a melding of the souls, the psyches, that hid behind a veneer of dislike, distrust, belligerence, even outward indifference. But we always knew, the two of us, that someday we'd come together the way we did, in hot, soul-searing passion. In the end, our love for each other simply couldn't be denied anymore. I mean, the man is simply crazy about me. It was just, you know, like, inevitable."

Cassandra rolled her eyes, wincing. What the hell was that load of baloney—a cross between a psychology textbook and a bad teenage slasher movie? Gotta have the gushy kids, gotta have some sex, some sort of moral "lesson" to get past the ratings board—

and then Freddie could jump out of the bushes and start slashing? Substitute a mud slide for some grinning monster with ten-inch fingernails, and that's what she had.

Pitiful. Just pitiful.

"And not a moment of this personal pity party is helping Jason one little bit," she grumbled. Her last sight of the boy, as he'd bolted down the street as if a runaway bull was charging after him, appeared once more before her eyes, so she dropped her forehead into her hands.

It was bad enough that Jason had a crush on her. She should have known that sooner, seen the signs, realized that. Although he visited her with the rest of the kids, he often found excuses to come over to her house on his own.

This "punishment" of writing several reports for her over the summer, well, it was simply the worst choice she could have made. Jason hadn't been upset when she'd told him about it, and now she knew why. Why, he might even have viewed it as her attempt to see more of him!

But to be found kissing his father? Oh, that went way beyond unfortunate, or badly planned, or potentially harmful. Jason had a crush on her—now he *was* crushed. Disillusioned, disappointed, displaced once again.

"I can't have anything to myself, can I, Dad? Not anything...or anybody."

Would she ever forget those words? Would she ever forget how devastated Jason had looked as he'd spoken them?

She couldn't see Sean again. Just couldn't. It was too dangerous. Heaven only knew how Jason would react.

That was, if the boy ever spoke to her again. If they ever could get to the point where he began to trust her again.

Cassandra stood and went to the counter, searching in the drawer until she found a plastic cover for the soda can. She couldn't drink the soda. She couldn't drink anything. Couldn't swallow.

She replaced the can in the refrigerator and started for the stairs, then remembered the light under her office door and retraced her steps. With her hand on the doorknob, she remembered the last time she had opened this door—only a few short hours ago, a life-time ago—and danced inside. Now her steps were dragging, old, tired.

Until she saw the lumpy-looking afghan on her father's worn leather couch, and the tousle of too-long hair on her mother's favorite cross-stitched pillow.

"Jason," she breathed softly, almost inaudibly. Her bottom lip trembled as tears stung at her eyes.

She turned, leaving him where he was, sound asleep, his face so young, so peaceful, and left the office, turning out the light, closing the door behind her and raising a silent thanks that she had, yet again, forgotten to lock her front door.

She'd phone Sean from her bedroom, reassure him about his son's whereabouts, talk him into waiting until morning and convince him to let Jason come home on his own.

Maybe it wasn't too late.

For any of them.

Sean stood at his second-floor office window a few minutes before nine, watching as his son walked up the cement path to the front door of the building. Jason was wearing sneakers, faded jeans and a white dress shirt, his tie rather crooked, his sport coat a little too short in the sleeves. He had his hair slicked back into a neat ponytail at his nape, and his hair looked wet, as if he hadn't bothered to dry it once he'd gotten out of the shower.

But he was there, he was on time, and Sean was feeling damn proud of him.

Sean had come home around five that morning after a night spent searching for his son, to see the light on his answering machine blinking, to hear Cassandra's four messages about Jason. *He's here, sound asleep. Don't come. He'll be fine. We'll work this out.*

It had been the same anxious message each time, each one a little more frantic, each one ending with, "Sean? Where *are* you?"

Sean hadn't called her back. How could he, with Jason sleeping in her office, not ten feet away from her telephone? It was enough that his son was safe, in one piece. It had to be enough.

Crossing to his desk, he picked up his telephone now and dialed Cassandra's number without having to look it up. "He's here," he said when she answered on the first ring, as if she'd been sitting with the telephone in her lap, which she probably had been.

He could hear her expelled sigh of relief. "I waited

upstairs until I heard the front door close, not wanting him to think he had to say anything, that either of us had to say anything, at least not until he's ready. He left a note on the kitchen table.''

''Really? A love letter, perhaps?'' Sean bit out, then mentally kicked himself. ''I'm sorry,'' he said quickly, sincerely. ''I haven't slept, and my mouth moved before I could think. I came into the office early this morning, planning to get a couple of things out of the way that couldn't be postponed, then come over to see you. Jason must have waited for me to leave, then come into the house to shower and dress for work.''

''He's trying to be responsible, Sean.''

Sean smiled into the receiver, still so damn glad Jason was all right that, for the moment at least, he could forgive almost anything. ''Responsible, huh? Yeah, well, I'll give him that. But his wardrobe needs work. What did he say in the note—or would you rather not break Jason's confidence?''

''As the note was addressed to the two of us, I'd already planned to read it to you,'' Cassandra answered, and Sean could hear the tension in her voice. ''It begins with an apology.

Sorry I didn't knock. Hope you don't mind that I crashed here, but I couldn't go home. Please tell Dad I'll be staying at Mom's for a couple of days, just until things cool off, you know. She's picking me up after work and says she'll loan me her car so I can get to work and stuff. See you around sometime, if that's all right.

"That's it, Sean. That, and the finished report on glazing. He had it stacked next to the computer, as if he'd worked on it most of the night."

Sean held the receiver away from his mouth for a moment so Cassandra wouldn't hear the short expletive he couldn't suppress. "He called Sally? Oh, I'll bet she's just loving this. Slaying the fatted calf, welcoming home the prodigal son, getting ready to spoil him rotten again. Hey, Jase, sure, come on home to mommy and mommy's car and mommy looking the other way when you come home at two in the morning—if you come home at all. Damn it!"

"Sean, you're overreacting and you know it. Where else would Jason go, if not to his mother? I think you two do need a small break from each other, actually, as your relationship has been pretty intense these past months. He'll be back—he said so, and he's working at your place every day, so you'll know he's all right. Now, if you're not too tired or too busy, I have a favor to ask of you."

The woman sure had a way of getting his attention. "A favor?"

"My insurance man called and said the Jeep is considered a total loss. I have to start car-shopping. I *hate* shopping for cars, I hate trying to keep prices and options straight. I hate having to ask about undercoating and dealer-prep fees and sports-package options. Besides, I believe I want to pocket most of the insurance money, use it to have the house painted, perhaps, and just lease a car this time."

Sean smiled as he scooped up his own car keys from the desk and slid them into his pocket. If it weren't for Cassandra, he and Jason might be killing each other at this moment. And, much as he appreciated all her help, it was comforting to know she didn't have the answer to every question, that there were areas in which *he* could help her. "You're not supposed to admit that you don't understand this stuff, Cassandra. All by yourself, you're setting back the woman's movement by at least a dozen years."

"Oh, I *understand* it well enough," she countered.

As she spoke, he held the receiver between his chin and shoulder, stuffing papers into his briefcase, thinking he could work at home for the remainder of the day—*after* he'd done the "great, big strong man helps the poor female find her way through that scary automobile jungle out there" routine.

"You do?" he answered, feeling slightly wicked. "Okay. You say you want to lease a car, right? So, tell me—what's gap insurance?"

"Gap insurance is the coverage you demand the dealer include as part of his end of the deal—that he pay for it, in other words—to insure that, if you have an accident and the car is destroyed, or whatever, this insurance will kick in to cover the residual figure listed in your lease even if the car is not worth that much at the time of the accident. Otherwise, the difference between what the dealer figured the car would be worth at the end of the lease and what the insurance thinks it was worth after you wrap it around a tree comes out of your own pocket. Or something like that," she added, her voice trailing off, then growing stronger once more. "I just know I want it, I definitely should have it, and I want the dealer to pay for it. Well, am I right? I spent all of Sunday afternoon studying this stuff.''

"Studying, you say? Where?" He put the briefcase down, somehow knowing that there wasn't going to be any time in his day for something so mundane, so uninteresting, as work. Not when he was about to go car-shopping with yet another side of the intriguing, enchanting Cassandra Mercer. "Wait, let me guess— on the Internet?"

"Sort of. It was a teenager in Idaho who goes by the name of MagWheels, actually. A very nice boy who logged-on with an information highway network I use and told me all about everything I needed to know. Nerds will one day rule the planet, Sean,'' she teased. He could close his eyes and mentally see her pushing the glasses she didn't really need higher on the bridge of her unique, delectable nose. "So? Will you go with me?"

"I'm already halfway out the door," he answered, hanging up the phone and heading for Ms. Finley's office, to tell her he wouldn't be in the office until the following day. She'd probably screw up her features, look at him disapprovingly, and then say, "Very well, sir."

The woman didn't disappoint him, adding, "Although I must say, sir, that this week's disruptions to our usual orderly routine are most distressing, as well as totally out of character for you. Sir."

Sean almost breezed through the secretary's office without stopping but, as he reached the doorway, he was suddenly struck by the need to have Ms. Finley answer a question for him. "Ms. Finley—Grace—were you a nerd in high school?"

"I beg your pardon, sir," the woman said, bristling. "And, furthermore, I believe that question crosses the unwritten boundary between employer and employee that I have striven so diligently to protect since the first day of my employment with this firm. Why, I—"

Sean crossed to the woman's desk, laying his palms on the pristine wooden surface as he leaned closer to her. "Were you a nerd, Grace?" he repeated. "A misfit. Too fat or too thin, too short or too tall, zits, braces, good grades, few friends, lousy social life? Unhappy, misunderstood, miserable?"

She avoided his eyes. "Well, I…that is…um…" She took a deep breath, then released it in a rush. "Yes, sir, Mr. Frame. I was, am, a nerd. Grade-A, Number One Nerd. And I *hate* it!"

"Grace," Sean said as he watched the woman's face coloring, noticing that her hair, always scraped back in a bun, was actually quite a lovely shade of honey-blond, "I'm giving you a two-week vacation, with pay. Starting the moment you cancel all my own appointments for the next two weeks."

She looked up at him through her incredibly unattractive thick-lensed glasses. Her eyes were mud brown, but they were sort of tilted at the corners. Not bad. Not too bad at all. But still, the woman wasn't quite a beauty at about thirty, and probably had been less than a beauty at eighteen. He stopped himself from asking what sort of underwear she sported beneath her stiff business suits. "But I had my vacation in April, sir. Two weeks."

"Where did you go?" Sean asked, realizing that he knew nothing, less than nothing, about this efficient, intelligent, colorless woman who'd worked for him for the past five years. "San Francisco? Las Vegas?"

"Trenton, sir," she answered, lifting her hand to fiddle with the cameo pin at the neck of her fully buttoned-up white blouse. She had lovely hands—long, thin fingers, neatly rounded nails. And those nails were painted a bright, sexy red! Why had he never noticed the woman's hands, the woman's nails? "That's in New Jersey. My brother lives there. I baby-sat his three children while he and his wife went to Paris."

"Of course you did," Sean answered, pushing himself away from the desk. "Well, now you're going to go to Paris, Grace. Paris, Rome, Vegas—wherever in the world you want to go. Start here, though, at one of those boutiques in the mall. A boutique, the beauty shop, the eye doctor's office for contact lenses, if you want—whatever and wherever the hell else you think you might need to do or go—and then you're off for Paris."

"San Diego," Ms. Finley said firmly, a small smile beginning to play around the corners of her usually tight-lipped mouth. "I have a cousin in San Diego, and she's been begging me to come visit for years, except I've always ended up baby-sitting for Fred's spoiled brats. She said her husband has this friend she wants me to meet…a doctor, I believe. He's supposedly very nice, and—"

"Perfect!" Sean all but shouted. "Two weeks in San Diego, Ms. Finley, and not a day less. Cancel those appointments, call down to the payroll office and have someone cut you a check for two weeks' pay—no! *three* weeks' pay—and then get your butt the hell out of here. That's an order!"

Grace was already reaching for the phone. "Yes, sir," she said as he turned for the doorway once more. "And congratulations, sir."

He sliced her a look over his shoulder. "Congratulations? For what?"

"I believe her name is Cassandra, sir? Cassandra Mercer? You know, that lovely woman who barged in here yesterday? Well, I thought so then, and I think so now. You'll make a lovely couple. Now, I imagine, all you have to do is convince Ms. Mercer of that fact."

Sean was dumbfounded. "Ms. Finley, there are depths to you that I have never, to this moment, fully appreciated."

She punched a few numbers into the phone, smiling at him. "Yes, sir. I know. I'll have flowers sent to Ms. Mercer's house before I leave. Have a nice vacation yourself, sir."

Sean shook his head, wondering how he had so lost himself along the way, so totally buried himself in his work, in his drive to get ahead, to stay ahead—in his need to *be* somebody. Was it any wonder he had never noticed his secretary, any wonder that his own son couldn't see him as anything more than the successful businessman when that was all he had shown to the world for so long?

"Thank you, Grace," he said, smiling. "We're *both* going to have nice vacations. Because I think we both damn well deserve them!"

"You can say that again," Grace grumbled into the receiver, then smiled and told the person on the other end to have a check ready for her in fifteen minutes.

Twelve

Cassandra put down her glass of soda with a slight thump of temper. "Because I don't *want* another Jeep, that's why! I've already had a Jeep, remember? Been there, done that—"

"Got the T-shirt," Sean finished for her. "I also remember. But a Jeep is a logical choice for this area of the country."

"Absolutely. But maybe I don't feel like being logical right now."

"It shows. A Jeep is also trustworthy, Cassandra."

Her temper cooled, and her sense of humor stepped up to the plate to take a swing or two. She liked this verbal sparring with Sean, and believed he enjoyed it as much as she did. "Trustworthy, huh? Again, a marvelous selling point, *Sean*. Although I will also *point* out that Boy Scouts are trustworthy, and I'm not contemplating buying one of them."

"Not funny. But, to continue. A Jeep is eminently reasonable."

She tried not to giggle as she saw the light of amusement, of challenge, in Sean's eyes. "True enough. I've never heard of an unreasonable Jeep. Go on, please. Hit me with some more sterling Jeep traits."

He leaned forward, his elbows on the tabletop. "All right. Try this one on for size. *Sturdy.*"

"Absolutely," she agreed, nodding sagely—at least she hoped she looked sage, whatever that was supposed to look like. "Strong as a bull."

"And practical."

"Practical? Whoops!" She pulled a comical face as she held out her hands in warning. "You may not want to go there, Sean. Now you're beginning to lose me."

"Too bad. Sensible!"

"Aha!" She pointed at Sean across the table, as if he had just said the magic word and a duck was going to come dropping down from the ceiling of The Saloon at any moment, two hundred dollars stuck in his mouth. "There—*there's* your answer! It's *sensible.* Who says I have to be sensible? I ask you, Sean, is your Mercedes *sensible?*"

"Now you're asking me to compare apples and oranges. My car is a simple matter of personal physical comfort. I just fit well in the Mercedes."

Cassandra couldn't suppress a bubble of laughter. "Well, jeez, of course you do, Sean. Who on earth wouldn't *fit well* in a Mercedes?"

He lifted his glass of beer and took a small drink. "I also own a four-wheel-drive vehicle, Cassandra. We live in Colorado, remember?"

"Show-off," she grumbled, sinking low on the banquette seating of the dim, cool and comfortable bar-restaurant they had entered ten minutes earlier, exhausted from three hours of shopping for the second-largest investment most Americans made, after they signed away most of their life on a home mortgage.

"I use the Mercedes for business, the Blazer for winter driving. But I need the Mercedes, Cassandra. It's important to keep a clear business image, a successful image, an—ah, hell, you're right. I'm a show-off."

His smile was so young, so unaffected, so dangerous to her equilibrium. And she was having more fun than she could remember having had in years. "Got ya!" she said triumphantly, lifting her soda glass in a mock toast to her own victory. Then she put it back down on the tabletop without drinking any of it and leaned forward, her elbows on the scattering of brochures she had picked up at the various dealerships. "Seriously, Sean, what do you think of the dark green one?"

"The green one?" His tone was soft, indulgent, amused. "Cassandra—you aren't going to pick a car because of its color, are you?"

"No. Of course not. It's just how I remember them, how I picture them in my mind." She felt warm, and cosseted, and so entirely female. Dressed in a flowered knee-length sundress she never would have worn to school, and strappy shoes she'd purchased on a whim the past fall at a closeout sale, her hair falling freely to her shoulders, her makeup light and summery, her glasses safely tucked in her purse, she knew she looked young, and feminine and—just perhaps— touchable.

And Sean seemed to think so, as well. He had, after all, walked into each showroom with his arm at her waist, and held open each car door for her as she sat behind the wheel of more automobiles, more makes, more models, than she could now possibly keep straight in her mind.

But he had stood back when any salesmen approached, allowing her to ask the questions, giving her space when she needed it, stepping in only when one uncomprehending salesman kept ignoring her and directing all his comments to him, instead. "I warned you, didn't I? Told you to talk to the lady," he'd asked rather tightly after the salesman had looked past her for a third time, answering her question, but concentrating on making sincere, heartfelt eye contact with Sean. "Cassandra, show him your checkbook."

She'd done as he asked, of course, barely able to keep from giggling, even though she'd been well on her way to becoming angry as the salesman had stubbornly continued to ignore her. "Here it is, Sean, all primed and ready to close a deal today. But not here, I don't believe. Nope. Definitely not here!"

And then, as the thick-headed salesman had stood there, his mouth dropped open, Sean had once more placed his hand at the back of her waist and walked her back to his Mercedes—and the two of them had collapsed against its sleek black hood, dissolved in laughter.

Oh, yes, so far it had been a wonderful, wonderful day.

Cassandra gathered up the brochures as the barmaid walked toward them, holding plates of hamburgers and french fries. "Do you suppose that salesman learned anything when we walked out on him?"

she asked as she eagerly pointed to the pickle chips on Sean's plate and he waved her off, quickly lifting both slices and popping them into his grinning mouth at the same time, just so that she couldn't steal them from him.

"If he didn't, he'll soon be looking for another line of work," Sean told her as she made short work of her own pickle slices. "I believe I read somewhere that more cars are bought by women these days than by men. Even more *Jeeps*."

"No Jeeps!" Cassandra countered, laughing. "Now, come on. Talk to me about the green one. Power steering, power brakes, front-wheel drive, a killer CD player. What else could I ask for?"

"A security system?"

"It has one. I checked. And electric windows, which are totally decadent. I do love electric windows."

"I've noticed," Sean said, signaling the barmaid with his empty glass.

Cassandra drew her top lip between her teeth, watching as the young woman brought him another draft beer.

"You want one?" he asked as the barmaid quickly disappeared again.

She shook her head, calling herself stupid for seeing two small glasses of beer as some sort of terrible thing. Sean obviously was only having a second glass because the day was unusually warm, and car shopping was thirsty work. There was no harm in it. No foul.

"No, thanks," she said, smiling. "I don't drink."

Then she nibbled on a french fry before saying, "Jason's okay, right? I mean, you said he showed up for work right on time this morning."

"Yes, he did. I'd like to think he has some sticking power, of course. And I called down to the payroll department early this morning, changing his name from Taylor to Frame. Otherwise, the kid won't be able to cash his paycheck on Friday. You say he's smart, and I agree, but I don't think he thought that one through."

Cassandra winced. "Neither did I. So everyone probably knows now that Sean is your son."

"He proved himself yesterday, Cassandra, when he caught that unnecessary complexity in our shipping-and-receiving software. I don't think he'll mind having Herb and the rest of them knowing he's the boss's son. Lord knows, I don't. I'm very, very proud of him."

"And you're going to tell him that, aren't you? That you're proud of him?"

She watched as Sean reached up with his left hand, scratching his right cheek, then rubbing his chin with his thumb and fingers. She used to hate when he did that at school board meetings. Now she thought the unconscious gesture endearing.

"When he comes home. When he lets me know it's okay to talk to him again. Yes. Then I'll talk to him, tell him. And then he'll bite off my head and go storming off to his room, or to your house—but at least I now know that's where he's going rather than his explanation as to his destination, which usually is the single word *out*. I'll yell after him, he'll slam the bedroom door or the front door behind him, and that will be that. Another day, another senseless confrontation. It's not much of a system, but it's ours. We've pretty much perfected it over the months. And it stinks, frankly.''

Cassandra reached across the table, taking his hand. ''I'm sorry. We were having such a pleasant day. I shouldn't have said anything.''

He returned the pressure of her fingers, and Cassandra felt heat rushing into her cheeks. She liked this man so much, after spending two years sticking pins in an imaginary voodoo doll of him stored in her brain. And here he was—part sophisticated businessman, part frightened orphan, part man of her dreams. Could she possibly have made love with him only a few short days ago? When she knew so little about him, when she longed to know so much more?

''I called Sally from my car on the way over to pick you up this morning,'' he told her, and she squeezed his hand again, then withdrew it. Clearly they were guidance counselor and parent again, and she wanted to retain at least a small part of her objectivity.

''Good,'' she said, nodding. ''Opening the lines of communication is always helpful.''

''You'd think so, wouldn't you?'' he answered, and his tone set off warning bells in her head.

''What happened?''

''She told me I'm a coldhearted bastard and always was,'' he said conversationally, although she could see a small muscle start to convulse in his cheek. ''I'm also a low-born, ungrateful, blood-sucking leech, in case you haven't figured that one out for yourself.''

Cassandra sat back against the cushions, frowning. "I'm missing something here, aren't I?"

"You could say that. Do you really want to hear True Confessions?"

"If you think it might help Jason, help the two of us in our dealings with him, then, yes. And if you don't mind telling me."

"How about I just tell you, and then we can decide what to do with the information, okay?"

Cassandra nodded, unable to trust her voice. She didn't know who she was right now, which hat she should be wearing, which role she should be playing. She did her best to be the competent guidance counselor, to have her mind involved, but not her emotions.

She doubted she'd have much success, then looked up at Sean, and knew she'd been right.

His smile was sad, breaking her heart, robbing her of all objectivity.

"Sally became pregnant the month before our high school graduation," he began, and Cassandra closed her eyes again, not wanting to hear any more, not wanting to picture either Sean or his ex-wife in that most terrible, most frightening situation—their lives just about to begin and feeling as if those lives were already over.

He cleared his throat quietly, then continued, "Phil Roberts, Sally's father, made sure we were married immediately, made sure we both went off to college. I had earned my football scholarship, yes, but I had to give it up when we got married, which is something I don't like to think about, much less tell people. Sally dropped out in her second year, saying she had never wanted to go to school, anyway, and went home to live with dearest Mommy and Daddy, when she wasn't jetting off somewhere with a new *friend,* that is. Jason had already been living with her parents, you understand, being taken care of by the nanny Phil had hired.''

"There was money, then," Cassandra interrupted quietly. "At least Jason was in a good home."

"If you say so," Sean said, sighing. "I know I tried to tell myself that was true, that Sally was just young, not spoiled rotten—that Jason wouldn't be spoiled rotten in turn." He pushed his plate away, never having taken a single bite of his hamburger, or another drink of beer. "I played my football, graduated with honors and came home to join Phil in the family business. The marriage was as good as over by then—not that there was much of a marriage there to begin with—but we played the game for another two years, until Jason was in school."

"And then you struck out on your own?" Cassandra remembered the name of Sean's business— R & F Associates, Incorporated—and wondered, just for a moment, if there was still something she wasn't seeing.

He shook his head. "No. Then Sally and I divorced and I damn near lived on the job. I slept in a one-room firetrap and saved every cent I made, invested it in company stock. I doubled, then tripled the company's profits, and looked up one day to see that I was a fairly wealthy man. Phil's the R in R & F, but he hadn't been active in the company since I proved to him that I could do the job for him. He was simply too busy with his skiing, and his horse racing, and his summers in Miami—that sort of thing.''

He stopped speaking for a moment, took a sip of the now warm beer. ''Then,'' he went on, still with the curious monotone he'd been using to explain his life history, ''with my stock purchases and three of the other major stockholders to back me, I pushed my way to the top of the ladder. Last year I bought out Phil's shares completely, but I'm keeping the company name, as it was already well-known and another change would have only confused things. As I've already admitted, Cassandra, I'm ambitious. Or a miserable, coldhearted bastard, depending on who is doing the describing. Oh, one more thing. Jason doesn't know it, but he's working for himself, as I've already signed over thirty-four percent of the company, the last of Phil's old shares, to him.''

Cassandra sat very still, trying to absorb everything Sean had said. And she came up with an intriguing conclusion. ''I'm going to lease the green one,'' she said, gathering up the brochures as the barmaid returned to hand Sean the check.

He paid the woman immediately, then glared at Cassandra. ''That's it? I bare my soul, tell you things I don't like hearing much less sharing, and you say, 'I'm going to lease the green one'?''

She put down the stack of brochures. ''Look, Sean,'' she began, trying to explain. ''You don't need me to tell you that you and Sally married for all the wrong reasons and then lucked out by ending up with one very special, wonderful kid. Right? You don't need me to tell you that ending your marriage was probably a good thing for the two of you—maybe for the three of you. And you certainly don't need my opinion on how you came to own your business, because that has absolutely nothing to do with how I handle Jason. Right again?"

"Go on."

The heat of his gaze was making her uncomfortable. "You want to know what I got out of all of this, don't you?"

"That was the point of this conversation, wasn't it?"

She cleared her throat, then stood up, wishing herself out of The Saloon, wishing herself out of Colorado. Kansas was a nice place, she'd heard. "Yes," she said as they stepped out into the sunlight, squinting after the darkness inside the bar. "That was the point."

"And you've reached some conclusions?"

Don't push, don't push, she warned silently as he opened the car door for her and she slid into the front seat, then waited for him to walk around the car and climb behind the wheel. "You're right. You do fit well in a Mercedes," she said as he started the engine and they headed back toward the dealership where the green car waited.

"Yes, well—" she braved on when his only answer was another tight-lipped glare "—as I was saying. Or not saying, as the case may be... Oh, hell, Sean, don't you see it?"

He put on the turn signal and maneuvered the car into the left lane. "No, damn it, I don't see it—because you haven't said a word about what *it* is!"

She clasped her hands together in her lap, trying to physically push her thoughts together, mold them, make them into something he would not only understand but would not throw her out of the car for saying to him. "You look at Jason and see everything flighty and spoiled about Sally, maybe even about Phil, as well. You see the privilege he's had since his birth, as compared to your own difficult struggle. And, at the same time you're condemning him for his mother's sins, you're scared to death he might recreate your own as well and become that coldhearted bastard you say Sally believes you to be."

"That's ridiculous! And, before you say it, I certainly don't see Jason as some wild kid who'd end up impregnating the nearest cheerleader."

"I'm not talking about that sin, Sean, if sin is what you want to call it, and I don't, by the way. I call that an error in judgment," Cassandra explained quietly. "I'm talking about this coldhearted bastard Sally has termed you, this man who can't give love or accept love, because it always had a price tag, and it always could be taken away."

"Now you're being more than ridiculous," Sean said, pulling onto the car lot.

"Am I? You told me Sally spoils Jason, showers him with presents and the like, right?"

"I told you that, yes."

"That isn't love, Sean. Neither is riding herd on the kid as if he was going to do something wrong if

you looked away from him for a second. Sally ma-
nipulated Jason with gifts and privileges, and he soon
learned how to use his behavior to manipulate *her*.
At the same time, you were off building your career,
admitting to just about living at the office, so that
Jason really didn't have a father.''

''I wanted him to have stability. The stability I
never had. The same bed to come home to each night,
the same set of faces at the breakfast table.''

''Of course,'' Cassandra agreed. ''That's totally
understandable. But Jason has spent most of his life,
in my opinion, trying to get you to notice him. Good
grades didn't do it. Good behavior didn't do it. But
bad behavior worked wonders with his mother. You
didn't exactly say so, but I'm willing to believe that
a tantrum got him a new tricycle, and a bigger tantrum got him his own car. It wasn't love, perhaps, but
life certainly had its perks.''

''Go on,'' Sean said, turning off the engine as they
sat parked on a corner of the lot.

''You saw the good grades, and accepted them as
expected. You saw the car, the *things,* and saw your
son going down the same road Sally had taken. But
Jason caused *you* no trouble, so you were content to
leave him with Sally and go about building your company. Except Sally got married again. Sally had a new
husband and a new baby. And Jason was reduced to
the role of excess baggage. The old perks, the *things,*
suddenly didn't have the same appeal. He wanted
what he'd always wanted but had never before realized—he wanted *love.* He started staying out late,
started causing trouble, so that Sally contacted you

and asked for help. At that point, instead of indulging him, or ignoring him, you and Sally finally had to *deal* with him.''

''And I brought him here to Grand Springs, enrolled him in school, took away his toys and expected him to continue to get good grades, to make new friends, to *behave*. At which point,'' Sean said sadly, ''his grades started to slip, he began playing hooky, and he ended up breaking a dozen windows in the gymnasium. If you're going to try to get your father's attention, what better way to do it than by creating trouble for the old man who just happens to serve on the school board. Is that what you're saying?''

''There're a lot of windows in Grand Springs, Sean,'' Cassandra pointed out thoughtfully. ''I don't think it's a coincidence that he broke those particular windows. Although I still can't believe he did that. I also can't believe I keep *saying* that, but it just doesn't fit Jason's personality. He's acting out, yes. He wants your attention, your love, your acceptance, definitely. He longs to be understood for who he is. But he isn't the sort to go around destroying other people's property. He just isn't.''

''The janitor found Jason's sociology notebook in the grass outside the gym, remember? Right next to the spot where those river stones used to be arranged around the flagpole?''

''Jason didn't deny breaking the windows when the principal and I confronted him with the evidence and you were called in,'' Cassandra said, rubbing at her eyes with her thumb and forefinger. When had she gotten this pounding headache?

Sean took his hands off the steering wheel and held them in the air. "Whoa, let's back up a minute here. Are you saying Jason admitted breaking the windows, or just that he didn't *deny* breaking them?"

Cassandra rubbed at her eyes again, trying to think back to the meeting with the principal. "Mr. Cummings called Jason in and showed him the notebook, asked him to identify it. Then he told Jason that the windows had been broken and…and Jason just sat there, looking at me. I—I remember thinking that he looked rather disappointed in me, in the both of us. But he didn't deny breaking the windows."

She turned sideways on the seat, hesitating only long enough to unbuckle the constricting seat belt so that she could turn and look at Sean intently. "Then you came racing in, and you asked Jason what was going on, what he'd done wrong *this* time, and—"

"And Jason told me to ask Mr. Cummings, which I did, and Jim held up Jason's notebook. End of story."

"Oh, my God! Sean! Do you suppose—"

Sean slammed a fist against the steering wheel, so that Cassandra flinched, taken aback by his sudden anger. "What the hell's the *matter* with that kid?" he asked, but she knew he didn't really expect an answer from her. "It's as if he *wants* me to think the worst of him!"

Cassandra was out of her depth, and she knew it. "Perhaps if you and Jason were to seek out some family counseling, a psychologist trained in this sort of thing?" she offered, allowing her voice to trail off helplessly as Sean glared at her.

"Oh, really, Ms. Mercer?" he said, his tone not only angry, but bitingly sarcastic. "That's cute, you know. Really cute. You don't have the faintest idea what's going on, do you? How could you, when you're living your second childhood through *my* son? You open this can of worms, and then you go back and punt when the going gets tough. Here's your screwed-up kid, Mr. Frame. Now, you deal with him!"

"Sean, that's not what I meant at all. You're over-reacting—"

"There it is again! That marvelous word you use so often and so well. *Overreacting!* Yep, that's me all right. Well, guess what, Ms. Mercer? I'm going to overreact again. There's the door. The green car is waiting for you."

"Sean?"

"Oh, come on, you know what I mean. Find your own way home. And, while you're at it—see if you can find your way out of my life, my son's life. All right? Because right now I'm going back to work, picking up my son, and the two of us are going away for a few days, to my condo in Vail. Together. Where we can talk without him having a handy hiding place to go running to—either to his mother, or you."

Cassandra's eyes stung with unshed tears. "I—I think that would probably be best," she said, her voice breaking even as she struggled to compose herself. She gathered up her purse and the brochures, and put a trembling hand on the door handle.

Sean took hold of her arm, holding her in her seat.

"There's still something else to be resolved between us, Cassandra. Remember? This isn't over."

She felt hot color run into her cheeks, and nodded, unwilling to trust her voice.

"God!" Sean gritted the word out, pulling her against him so that her face was buried against his chest. "You drive me crazy! Don't ever stop saying what's on your mind, Cassandra, no matter how much I growl at you, all right? Because of you, in spite of my own stupidity, I just might have a chance to get through to that son of mine. I'm sorry, Cassandra. If my ego is smarting because I couldn't see my own mistakes, it's no reason to take my anger out on you."

If he could be honest, so could she, Cassandra decided. "You're right," she said, speaking against his shirt. "It's no excuse. And you frightened me, Sean, because I don't think I want to be out of your life, out of Jason's life."

"And I'd be an idiot to let you go." He bent down and kissed the top of her head. "Now, go lease that green car with the nifty electric windows, okay? And I'll see you Saturday night."

She mumbled against his chest again. "You will?" She took a deep breath, breathing in the scent of his aftershave, then released it slowly. "Why?"

Sean laughed out loud, and she heard the deep chuckle through his shirt. "Oh, Cassandra. We do have a long way to go, don't we, before all three of us graduate from our own private high schools and look life straight in the eye?"

She lifted her head, looked up into his eyes. "I'll be looking forward to Graduation Day," she said, then averted her gaze as she realized how candidly she had spoken, how much she had said in those few words.

He ran a finger down the length of her nose. ''And I'll be right there with you as we get our diplomas, probably going crazy wondering what sort of lacy nonsense you have on under that cumbersome cap and gown.''

Cassandra didn't know what to say. She had never played word games about sex, had no experience to draw on. ''Saturday?'' was all she could muster, and the question came out in a small squeak.

''Saturday,'' Sean answered. Cassandra opened the door and all but tumbled out of the car, standing on the lot, the brochures clutched to her chest, as she watched the Mercedes drive away.

Thirteen

There was a quote somewhere about the best-laid plans of mice and men and how they sometimes get royally screwed up—but Sean wasn't interested in quotes. He was interested in Jason. And Jason might have decided to come home, but he wasn't having any part of a getaway to Vail and a couple of days of father-son talks.

And the devil of it was that Sean really couldn't blame the kid. He was having a ball working at R & F, and he didn't want to miss a single day.

"But we'll talk, Dad," Jason had promised half-heartedly as he headed up the stairs to look through the pile of papers he'd brought home from the office. "Honest. You go have a great time in Vail. I'll be fine here. Really. It's much better here, without the hour commute from Mom's house."

Which, Sean realized as he walked into the living room and sat down in his favorite chair, left him with little to do for the next two weeks except sit here, staring at four walls, or go back to work.

And he wasn't going to go back to work.

Not when he hadn't had a vacation in five years. Not when he wanted, needed, to be with his son. And not when Cassandra's school year was over and the woman had as much free time as he did.

Sean looked up as Jason came back down the stairs, a Hootie and the Blowfish T-shirt replacing the white dress shirt he'd had on earlier, his long legs encased in a more decrepit pair of jeans. He sure was a handsome kid, even if he didn't exactly resemble any parental description of "clean-cut." Not in that outfit!

"Where are you going, son?" Sean called out as casually as possible as he rose from his chair and slowly walked toward the foyer.

"Out," Jason replied guardedly, his eyes on the tile floor, his posture going stiff, as if he was preparing himself for the inevitable battle such a response usually incited. They might have made it through Jason's return to the house and the discussion of a vacation in Vail without too much hassle, but Jason obviously believed that the explosion he'd expected earlier was now about to arrive.

"All right," Sean said, gesturing toward the living room. "But could we talk first? I have something I want to say to you, if you don't mind."

"Um, look, Dad, if you're going to try getting me to go to Vail again, I thought I already told you—I'm not going anywhere. I mean, I'm having *fun* for the first time in so long, doing something really *important,* and now you're trying to screw it all up with this business about father-and-son bonding, or whatever you were carrying on about. I mean, for crying out loud, Dad, can't I ever—"

"Jason!" Sean said, just a little too loudly, then held out his hands as he shook his head, as if physically pushing away yet another explosive argument. "Nope. No way, bucko, no how. Jason, I'm not going to let it be that easy for you. You say something smart-mouthed, I yell, and you get to storm out. Well, we're not going to play that game anymore."

Jason raised his head and looked at his father. "We're not?"

"No," Sean answered, smiling. "Although we have gotten it pretty well down to a science, I'll have to admit. What we're going to do, son, is sit down in the living room and *talk* to each other. You'll talk to me, and I'll listen. I'll talk to you, and you'll listen. Me first, of course. Age does have its privileges."

"Figures," Jason muttered, but he shuffled into the living room, anyway, his hands stuck deep in his pockets. He sat down on the piano bench, well away from the arrangement of comfortable chairs and couch, well away from his father. "Okay, Dad. You first."

Sean had undergone less painful root canals, but he decided the only thing he could do was to suck up this particular pain and get on with it. He sat down on the edge of the couch, his elbows on his knees, and looked across the room at his prickly son. He decided to keep it short and sweet, and get right to the point. "I want to tell you how proud I am of you, Jason. You're doing a great job down at R & F."

Sean shifted his eyes from side to side, as if looking around to see if the living room had secretly been transported to the Twilight Zone. "You're kidding, right?" he said after a moment, a nervous smile playing around his lips.

"No Jason, I'm not kidding," Sean said, wishing it didn't hurt so much to see Jason's surprise. Had his compliments to his son been so few, so rare, that he couldn't believe one when he heard it? "I saw what you did with the software program, and you were right on. You're saving the company a good deal of time and money."

Jason scratched the back of his head. "Yeah, well, it was an okay start, but there were a couple of things I hadn't thought about, you know. I mean, Herb thought it was good, but then Jerry pointed out a couple of places where my changes could really screw up the works. But we've been working on them all day today, and…"

Sean leaned forward as Jason continued to talk about his workday, watching his son's animated features, seeing the same flare of fire and avid interest he himself had once felt for his work, back when he was young, and hungry, and believed the whole, great, wide world could be conquered if you just wanted to badly enough.

"But that might work better if you can interface it with the software from the different overnight services, taking into account varying fees for one- and two-day delivery," Sean said after a while, hopefully helpfully, and Jason stood up quickly, as if he couldn't keep still, and walked across the room, to sit down on the chair directly opposite Sean's.

"Yeah, that's what Jerry said," Jason added, his eyes shining. "Then you have to factor in costs for Saturday delivery and staff overtime and…"

They talked for twenty minutes. Twenty minutes

with no shouting, no finger-pointing, no uncomfortable silences, no accusations.

It was wonderful. Beyond wonderful. And Jason was one hell of a nice kid. Just the sort of kid you'd want for one of your own.

And he was Sean's own.

He couldn't hide his smile when Jason stood up at last, saying, "I was just going out for a pizza, you know, and then maybe hack around at the mall for an hour or so, to look for a new sport coat for work. You want to come along?"

Did Sean want to come along? Oh, yeah. He did.

He reached in his pocket and pulled out the small black rectangle that was the key to his Mercedes, then flipped it across the room to Jason, who automatically snagged it out of the air. "You drive, all right?"

"The Mercedes?" Jason's face lit up like the proverbial Christmas tree. "You're kidding!"

"Nope. I'm not kidding. You drive, I pick the radio station. Agreed?"

Jason's grin widened. "I'd agree to anything if you'll let me drive the Mercedes."

Sean almost opened his mouth and asked, "Would you agree to talking about that day in Jim Cummings' office, when you let us all believe you broke the gym windows?" But he didn't, because he didn't want to ruin this moment and knew that those words would explode this small island of communication with the force of a nuclear explosion on Bikini Island.

"I'll just get rid of this shirt and tie and meet you out front," Sean said, heading for the stairs and wishing he had time to call Cassandra and tell her how well things were going—like a dog who had just learned a new trick and now wanted a pat on the head.

"Hey, Jase?" he asked impulsively, turning on the third step and stopping his son just as he was heading out the front door. "After we hit the mall and find that new sport coat, do you want to call Ms. Mercer and see if she wants to meet us somewhere for ice cream?"

Jason was silent for a few moments, during which Sean suffered the tortures of the big-mouthed. "Sure," he said then, nodding his head. "Yeah, okay. That's cool."

"All right!" Sean said, relieved, and turned once more, heading up the stairs two at a time.

Some pizza. Some shopping—for a couple of sport coats, some decent slacks, a few good shirts. And then, to top off the evening, sitting across a table from Cassandra Mercer, going quietly out of his mind as he watched her lick chocolate fudge topping off a long-handled spoon.

Oh, yeah. It was going to be a great night. A really great night! And the hell with that best-laid plans of mice and men stuff....

"Festus! Don't even think about it!"

The cat, who had been about to touch a front paw to the partially open rosebud—probably intending to swat at it as if it were a new toy—shot Cassandra a dirty look and then hopped down from the tabletop as if losing interest in the towering vase of flowers.

Cassandra, however, was still utterly fascinated by them. She had come home, driving her brand-new green car, to find Tammy Lutton sitting on her front porch, the long white florist's box across her lap as she pushed herself back and forth on the old metal glider that had belonged to Professor Mercer.

"I was just coming up the walk when the delivery van stopped," Tammy had explained, "so I told the guy I'd make sure you got them. You owe me a dollar for his tip. You did want to tip him, didn't you? They're roses, a dozen of them. Gorgeous deep red ones. I knew you wouldn't mind if I peeked. You don't mind, do you?"

Cassandra hadn't minded. She had been way too curious to see if there was a card with the flowers, and had only opened the front door and ushered Tammy, and the florist's box, inside. Flowers! When had been the last time she'd gotten flowers? Too long ago to remember, that was for sure!

Tammy had stayed for more than an hour, admiring the new car, then asking Cassandra's advice on an argument she was having with her friend, Matt, over the merits of a summer spent taking an accelerated computer course at Burke or a month spent white-water rafting with her older brother and three of his college mates from Virginia.

Matt, who had an enormous crush on Tammy—not that Tammy realized it—had quite obviously come down favoring the computer course, and Tammy was torn between being responsible and having a good time.

After sneaking a quick look at the card enclosed with the flowers, and seeing the words "Love, Sean" typed on the small card, Cassandra had enlisted

Tammy to arrange the flowers in a vase they'd unearthed from beneath the sink, then turned herself
away from thoughts of Sean and forced herself back
into guidance counselor mode.

"We'll use the time-honored method, Tammy,"
she'd said to the girl, opening a drawer and pulling
out a pad of paper and a pencil. "Draw a line down
the center of the page and head the two columns with
Vacation and Computer Course."

The girl had pushed her long auburn hair—streaked
with gold this week, Cassandra had noticed—out of
her face and grinned. "I know the drill, Ms. Mercer.
You want me to do pros and cons. Why I should go
with Frank and his roommates on one side, and why
I should stay here in Grand Springs and take the computer course on the other. I've already done that, and
thrown away the paper. And I still want to go with
Frank. My parents say it's up to me, but Matt said I
should talk to you."

Cassandra had pulled two soda cans from the re-
frigerator, popped the tops and handed one can to
Tammy as she sat down at the kitchen table. "Oh.
Okay. In other words, Tammy, you're not here to talk
about this. You're here to make Matt happy, and so
I can rubber-stamp your decision, right?"

Tammy shook her head, and Cassandra watched as
the curtain of streaked hair came down over the
young face once more. "No," she said, sighing. "I'm
here so you can talk me out of going. The way you
talked Jason out of leaving school last October and
going home to his mother without really giving Burke
a shot. The way you listened to him when he told us

how he wanted to go out for place kicker on the football team. The way you convinced Matt that losing the election for class president wasn't half the defeat it would have been if he hadn't had the guts to run for the office in the first place. You see what I mean, Ms. Mercer? I want you to convince me to do the right thing. And,'' she had ended, sighing, ''the right thing is for me to stay home and take the course. I mean, I'd get college credit and everything.''

Cassandra smiled now as she moved the vase of roses for the fifth time, this time trying out how it looked on top of her mother's mahogany credenza in the dining room, and remembered what she had said to Tammy.

Because, just as she had been about to do as the girl had asked—reinforce all the reasons why the computer course was the sensible, sane, responsible thing to do—she had looked out the kitchen window and seen her lovely new green car. The one with the nifty ''spoiler'' on the back and all those nonessential sports package options she hadn't really needed.

''You can always take a computer course, Tammy,'' she had told the surprised girl. ''Burke offers it again over Christmas vacation. But this summer will only be here this year. This trip will only be here this year. You and your brother will have only this summer to make a memory you'll share for a lifetime. So go for it, Tammy. Oh—and maybe drop a postcard to Matt once in a while, okay?''

Tammy had let out a squeal of teenage delight and hopped up to give Cassandra a hug and kiss before racing home to call her brother, and Cassandra had been left alone with her bloodred roses for company, wondering when she had lost her mind.

But had she? Being a guidance counselor wasn't all college choices and educational direction. There was a part of her job, a large part of her job, that had to do with guiding a teenager into becoming a whole person, a total person. And computer courses and college choices and preparation for SAT achievement exams certainly weren't all that were important to a developing mind, a maturing personality.

Though, she'd probably have to bake Matt some of his favorite peanut butter cookies to help convince him of that fact, she decided as she picked up the vase again, this time moving it to the living room and the coffee table in front of the couch. One thing she'd learned about roses—they looked good no matter where you put them.

Cassandra sat on the couch and leaned forward to sniff at the heady aroma of the flowers as she picked up the remote control and turned on the television in time for the nightly news. She'd been checking daily, hoping to hear news of Randi Howell, the girl the news people had dubbed "The Disappearing Bride."

She felt a kinship with the young woman, whom she was sure had made a last-moment decision to cancel her wedding and go off in search of something important to her. Independence, perhaps? A chance to make her own decisions? A life not bound by someone else's idea of what makes a happy woman?

Probably not. Cassandra had woven a fantasy about Randi Howell, and one that undoubtedly had nothing to do with the reason the bride had disappeared. But believing the young woman had gone off voluntarily was a lot easier to accept than to believe she might be in trouble—perhaps even kidnapped. Or perhaps—and this was worst of all—buried these many days under one of the mud slides.

Cassandra turned up the sound as the commercial for Squaw Creek Lodge—the very place from which Randi Howell had disappeared—ended and the news anchor began his rundown of the top stories for the day. There were still roads that remained closed on the outskirts of Grand Springs, and Cassandra watched videotape of bulldozers pushing rocks and workmen standing around watching the bulldozer pushing rocks.

That was followed by a story on young Victoria Sloane, the child who had been trapped in a cave during the mud slides. She was shown on screen with her parents, a handsome couple identified as Cassidy and Karen Sloane. Cassandra remembered that Karen Sloane was one of the doctors at Vanderbilt Memorial hospital, although her face didn't look familiar. Hadn't Sean said he knew her? She couldn't remember, but he probably did. Sean seemed to know everyone.

Cassandra frowned as she looked at Cassidy Sloane, who had the sort of black, brooding eyes that hid much more than they revealed, although at the moment they seemed to be saying quite clearly, "This is my child, and I won't allow anything, or anyone, to ever hurt her." She looked at Karen Sloane again, at her slender build, her expressive gray eyes, and wondered if she ever felt intimidated by this husband of hers.

"I'm getting fanciful," Cassandra said out loud as Festus hopped up on the couch and began butting his head against her thigh, which was his way of saying it was time she let him out for his evening prowl.

She put down the remote control and followed Festus to the front door, then returned in time to see more tape footage on the screen and listen to the news anchor giving a further update on the death of Mayor Olivia Stuart. Her son, Hal Stuart, was shown leaving the late mayor's home as the news anchor reported that the police were still investigating the mayor's death, which was still unofficially classified as due to a heart attack.

"You don't sound convinced," Cassandra said to the news anchor, who had already gone on to another story concerning structural damage to some of Grand Springs' homes and places of business, saying that teams of inspectors were still working to be sure none of the structures were uninhabitable.

She turned off the set as another commercial was being run, having decided that watching the news was nearly as good as watching regular programming— full of human stories and possible plot twists that kept you tuning in, hoping to learn more.

She also decided that she was doing everything she could to keep her mind occupied with other people's lives, other people's problems, so that she didn't have to confront her own.

Sean might have left her with a hug and some pretty tantalizing hints as to his feelings for her, but he had also left her with more questions than answers. Had she been trying to relive her high school days with Jason, and Tammy, and Matt, and the others? Had she been caught up in a spontaneous explosion of emotion last Friday night with Sean? Or had she been living out a decade-long fantasy where she was the cheerleader and Sean was the football captain who had taken her to a secluded spot for a little kissing, a little petting—a little daring that had gone too far, gotten out of hand?

Was she a grown woman, an educated woman, a responsible woman? Or was she a fanciful child who shouldn't be allowed out without a keeper?

She went upstairs, unbuttoning her blouse as she walked into her bedroom, then gathered up fresh underwear and headed for the shower. Just looking at the filmy ivory satin and lace of her bra and panties brought a faint blush to her cheeks. How she loved the feel of silk against her body, of satin. How she had loved, even more, the feel of Sean Frame's hands against her skin, his flesh pressed against hers.

Turning on the shower, she undressed completely and stood in front of the mirror over the sink. She looked at her reflection as she lifted her hair with both hands and piled it on top of her head, turning right and left, inspecting her image, taking in the sweep of her jaw, noticing the lift of her breasts as she held her arms high, her elbows bent.

Naked, she certainly didn't look like the daughter of the Professors Mercer, the shy, skinny, bespectacled schoolgirl who couldn't get a date, even for the Sadie Hawkins dance. Nor did she look like the confused college girl who had damn near flunked out of college, out of life.

She looked…she looked…how *did* she look? Young? Sensual? Eager? Ready to take on life? Ready to love? Ready to be loved?

Dropping her hands to her sides, she stepped back a few paces from the sink so that she could see more of her reflection in the mirror. The nip of her waist. The sweep of her hip. She lifted her hands to her waist, stroked her fingers across the bare skin, then raised her hands to cup her breasts.

Were they good breasts? Full enough? Certainly they were responsive enough, for even her slight touch now awoke sensations she hadn't known existed before Sean had shown her the delights his hands, mouth, teeth and tongue could elicit from a part of her anatomy she had never considered to be more than a nuisance, a necessary encumbrance.

She watched, her bottom lip caught between her teeth, as she drew her thumbs over her nipples, and the skin puckered, hardened, set off a sweet answering, curiously coiling sensation between her legs.

Did she want Sean, or did she want this strange new sensation?

She closed her eyes and slid her hands downward, over her rib cage, past her waist, onto the flare of her hips. Slowly, her fingers drew up into tight fists and she opened her eyes, smiling into the mirror. No. The sensation was good. The sensation was wonderful.

But it was nothing without Sean. Without his mouth against hers. Without his arms tight around her. Without his strength, his solidness, his whispered words that turned her bones to water. The smell of him. The taste of him.

His anger. His stubbornness. His deep-throated chuckle. His love for his son. His confusion, his pain, his sad childhood and the great strides he had made to build himself a life, to build a future for his son.

"You're in love with the man, Cassandra," she told herself, unsurprised to see that she had begun crying, that a single tear was, even now, slowly making its way down her cheek. "And, if he loves you back, you're going to become the Cassandra Mercer who has been hiding so long."

Which means you're going to have to tell him all of it, you know, her inner self reminded her as she stepped into the shower and let the full force of the spray wash over her heated body. *He told you. He came to you, bared his soul, told his story. Will you ever really be free to love him if you don't do the same?*

"I thought you went on vacation or something," Cassandra said out loud, wishing her inner voice in China or somewhere equally distant. "Can't we just take this one day at a time? Solve Jason's problems first? Get to know each other a little better?"

Nope. The longer you wait, the harder it will be. But you know that, don't you?

"Well, it doesn't matter, anyway," Cassandra told herself. "I may be in love with him, but he's far from in love with me. He might feel *responsible* for me after what happened, but that will go away soon enough when I can tell him I'm not pregnant. And he's grateful to me for helping with Jason, of course. But that doesn't mean he's in love with me.''

He sent you roses.

''His secretary probably sent them. For all I know, he sends roses to everyone. Probably has a standing account at the florist.''

''I'd be an idiot to let you go.'' Isn't that what he said, Cassandra? Aren't those words branded on your brain, on your heart?

''Stop it!'' she protested as she shoved a hand against the single handle, cutting off the flow of water. She shook her head, realizing that she had been talking to herself out loud. Sane people sang in the shower. They didn't hold conversations with themselves. And now, just to top it all off, she was hearing bells ringing.

Bells?

''The telephone!'' Grabbing a towel from the bar, she quickly wrapped its length around her dripping-wet body and ran into the bedroom, picking up the receiver just as it rang again. ''Yes—hello!'' she shouted breathlessly into the mouthpiece, just knowing that Sean was on the other end.

''Cassandra? I was just going to hang up.''

She subsided onto the bed, not caring that she was probably making a soggy mess of her bedspread. ''I was in the shower when I heard the phone,'' she said, curling her toes into the throw rug at her feet.

''In the shower? Interesting. And what are you wearing now? How do you look?''

She looked at the towel that was slipping from her breasts. ''How do you think I look, you idiot?'' she responded, feeling her skin grow hot. Yes, this was sexual banter. She might be new at the game, but it was one she was pretty sure she enjoyed.

"I'd tell you, but this is a family show," he said, laughing.

"A family show?"

"Just kidding. Look, we're at the mall, Jason and I. Buying him some new clothes that, believe it or not, don't come with holes already in the knees. Anyway, we were thinking that, maybe, if you're in the mood, you and your new car could meet us at the ice cream place in here. Say, in an hour or so? How long will it take for you to get dressed and get here?"

Cassandra ran a hand through her wet hair and mentally calculated how long it would take her to dry her hair, get dressed and drive to the mall. "Forty-five minutes, tops," she said. "It sounds like you two are getting along tonight?" she added hopefully, framing her words as a question and mentally crossing her fingers as she waited for his answer.

"We've had a great night, as a matter-of-fact. You wouldn't believe how great it has been, thanks mostly to you," Sean answered, then she heard him say something else, his mouth obviously moved away from the phone. "Look, Jason just remembered something else he wants to buy—a book about some new computer language. He's already nearly out of sight, so I'd better catch up with him. We'll see you later?"

She nodded, then remembered he couldn't see her and said, "Yes. I'll be there."

Sean chuckled.

"What?" she asked, confused.

"Oh, nothing," he answered, his voice suddenly soft and intimate. "I was just thinking about how jazzed Jason is going to be when I tell him he can have the Mercedes for the rest of the night, while you drive me home."

"You want me to drive you home tonight?" Cassandra's head was swimming.

"To *my* home? Eventually, Cassandra. Eventually. Let's just see how it goes, okay? Bye now!"

Cassandra held on to the receiver long after all she could hear was the dial tone buzzing in her ear. What a strange conversation! Why, if she was right, Sean had just invited himself back to her house tonight. She hopped up from the bed, straightening the bedspread, checking it with the flat of her hand to see how damp it might be.

The bed? What was she thinking? That he had invited himself to her house? To her bed?

Told ya so, her inner voice whispered, and, as Cassandra raced back to the bathroom to scoop up her underwear, she didn't care in the least that her inner voice was sounding insufferably smug.

Fourteen

"So? Is this Becky a nice girl?"

Cassandra turned away from the open cabinet and looked at Sean, who was sitting at the kitchen table. "Hmm?" she asked, only belatedly realizing she was pressing her lips together between her teeth. Where *was* the old bottle of brandy that had belonged to her father? "Becky?" she repeated, then smiled. "What's the matter, Sean? You worried that little freckle-faced redhead is going to turn into a femme fatale and work her feminine wiles on your poor, innocent little baby?"

"Jason's no baby, and I have a feeling he's pretty far from innocent, at least on the *theory* end of things. Not after the housekeeper brought me that copy of *Playboy* she found stuck between his mattress and box spring."

"Ouch!" Cassandra gave an exaggerated wince, then closed the cabinet door and went down on her haunches, to open the lower cabinets. "Burke has a wonderful sex education program, Sean, thanks to my two-year fight with certain people on the school board who wanted it removed from the curriculum," she said as she pushed the blender out of the way and looked into the dark corner of the cabinet, still searching for the brandy bottle. "But it doesn't include the more nifty props."

"Hey—I was on your side on that one, remember? As a matter-of-fact, I think mine was the deciding vote that retained the course."

She closed the cabinet doors, scooted to her left and opened the next cabinet. "Yes, I remember. Every time I wanted to hate you, you'd go and do something that made me have to thank you. Which made me hate you more. Darn it!" She sat back on the floor, rubbing at her head after hitting it against the top of the cabinet.

Sean leaned sideways on his chair and peered under the table at her. "I'd ask what in hell you're doing down there, but then you'd probably tell me, right?"

Cassandra scrambled to her feet, still rubbing at her head even as she gave the cabinet doors a kick, closing them. "I'm looking for my father's brandy," she explained grumpily even as he grinned at her. "It's all I have in the house."

"I don't need brandy, Cassandra," Sean answered, reaching to take a pretzel from the bowlful she had placed on the table. "I'll just take a beer, if that's all right. And, if you don't have any beer, a soda will do just as well."

"You're sure?" she asked, heading for the refrigerator and pulling out two soda cans. She popped the tops before he could answer, and then pulled two glasses from the cabinet beside the sink. "You'll want ice, of course?" she asked, heading back to the refrigerator once more.

"What I want, Cassandra, is for you to stop running around the kitchen and just sit down and talk to me,'' he told her, and she hesitated with her hand on the freezer handle, letting out her pent-up breath. ''Unless you want me to fix an ice pack for your head?''

''I'm sorry,'' she said, subsiding into a chair. ''I—I'm sort of nervous, if you want the truth.''

He reached across the table, taking her hand in both of his, stroking his thumb across her fingertips, lighting a small fire in her belly. ''Nothing's going to happen that you don't want to have happen, Cassandra. I promise. Just say the word and I can find my own way home.''

''No! I mean—no, that's all right,'' she said quickly. Too quickly. If only her heart would stop pounding so furiously. If only Sean would stop smiling at her, looking at her, touching her. ''Um—let's go into the living room, all right?'' she said, pulling her hand free and nearly jumping up from her chair.

He picked up the two soda cans and followed her down the hallway, into the darkened living room.

She flipped on a single light and saw the roses sitting on the coffee table. ''Oh, my gosh,'' she said, coming to a sudden halt, so that Sean bumped into her, spilling some soda down the back of her blouse.

''What's wrong?'' he asked, standing there with two dripping cans of soda and looking eminently adorable.

''I—I forgot to thank you for the flowers,'' she explained as she took the cans from him, cringing as she saw droplets of soda on his fingers, his tan slacks, his canvas sneakers. ''So, um, thank you. Thank you!

Oh, your clothing! Look what I've done! Stay there,''
she ordered, even as she headed for the kitchen, ''and
I'll get a wet cloth. I wouldn't want anything to stain
or anything.''

It was only when she was standing at the sink, wet-
ting a dish towel under the running faucet, and caught
a glimpse of her rattled-looking reflection in the
night-darkened windowpanes above the sink that her
bottom lip began to tremble.

What an idiot she was! A clumsy, bumbling, blath-
ering *idiot!* And with all the finesse, all the grace, all
the sexual confidence of the silly, repressed near-
virgin that she was. She couldn't handle a sexual encounter. She couldn't even handle the *preamble* to a
sexual encounter!

She'd been fine at the ice cream parlor. Well, almost fine. She'd ordered a chocolate marshmallow
and peanut sundae, and it had come with a cherry on
top. She didn't like cherries, never had, but Sean did.
She had already ''sensed'' that when he'd gotten a
cherry-vanilla sundae.

So she'd offered him the cherry from her sundae.
A simple enough gesture. Except he hadn't reached
over with his spoon and scooped it off the mountain
of whipped cream. Oh, no. That would have been too
easy. He'd simply opened his mouth and allowed her
to feed the cherry to him.

Her cheeks burned again now as she remembered
the way he had closed his lips around the cherry as
he looked at her, looked deeply into her eyes—and
as his hand had somehow come to rest on her thigh
at the same time.

Jason, oblivious to his lecherous father's under-the-table flirting, had continued to talk on and on about his great new sport coats, both of them, and the even greater ties he'd gotten to go with them, even digging into the plastic bags beside him on his side of the booth and pulling them out to show to her.

"Very nice," Cassandra remembered saying to him as Sean's hand had slid down to give her knee a gentle squeeze.

"Yes, very nice indeed," he'd echoed.

Oh, he was a cool one, he was. Able to keep up a conversation with Jason and with Becky, who had joined them at some point—Cassandra's memory was hazy on that point. Able to smile and joke and act just as if his left hand had never settled on her knee, her thigh, for the entire time they sat in the booth.

And then he had handed Jason the keys to the Mercedes! "Why don't you two see what's playing at the multiplex here at the mall?" he'd suggested as Jason looked at Becky, an unholy grin on his face.

He hadn't had to ask twice, of course. Jason and Becky were gone before Cassandra could so much as remind Jason that he had another report due to her in a few days, and she and Sean were left sitting, still side by side, with only a mountain of plastic bags left behind on the opposite side of the booth.

And now they were here. At her house. Together. Alone. Very much together. Very much alone. Unchaperoned. With hours and hours ahead of them before Jason's one o'clock curfew, when Sean most definitely should be home waiting for his son, back in his role of father.

And now here she was. At her house. In her kitchen. Staring at her reflection in a darkened window, and without a clue as to what should happen next.

"I think that towel is wet enough now," Sean said from behind her as he leaned over her shoulder and took the wet cloth from her nerveless fingers. "I already used some napkins to clean up most of the mess, although there wasn't much. Here, hold still, and I'll dab at the soda on your blouse."

"Oh, that's all right," Cassandra said quickly, automatically moving to turn off the faucet before turning around, just to have the sopping-wet cloth, and Sean's hand, collide with her breasts. She would have jumped backward, out of reach, except that she was already pressed up against the edge of the counter and had nowhere to go. She tried to smile but couldn't. She tried to look at him but knew she shouldn't.

Droplets of cool water ran down her skin, dampened her blouse, ran in sensual rivulets between her breasts.

His hand didn't move away from her. Instead, it moved closer. Higher. To the modest area of flesh exposed above the V-neck of her blouse. She felt the coolness of the wet towel against her heated skin, sliding toward her collarbone, along the column of her throat. It was blessedly cool, blessedly soothing and mind-shattering in its potential for pleasure.

"The—the stain is on the back of my blouse," she said weakly, fighting the impulse to shiver in unexpected delight. With sudden desire.

"I know," he told her as he leaned forward

slightly, his mouth at her temple, his sweet breath tickling her ear. "Does it matter?"

His hand moved again, and the top button of her blouse fell open. Then the second button. The cloth was still wet, but now it was beginning to warm from the heat of her body as Sean slowly drew it along the top edge of her bra—that sheer scrap of foolishness that now seemed so cumbersome, so restricting.

The cloth disappeared—Cassandra wasn't quite sure when, quite sure how—to be replaced by Sean's mouth, hot and wet against her damp cleavage. The pressure of his lower body, tight against her pelvis, was the only thing that kept her upright as all strength left her legs and all her blood rushed to her head, making her senses swim.

Her blouse hung loose from the waistband of her skirt, all the buttons open now. Sean's hands spanned her bare midriff, sending delicious sensations rippling along her nerve endings, dancing over her rib cage.

She couldn't control her breathing, which was becoming quick, and ragged, and increasingly shallow as she tried not to move, not wanting to miss a moment of sensation as Sean's mouth moved toward her left breast.

He didn't release the front closing of her bra, but rather ministered to her through the wisp of silk. The feelings she'd had for that fleeting moment earlier in the bathroom came back a thousandfold as his mouth found her, his tongue traced circles around her, his teeth—oh! his teeth!—gently nipped, teased, awakened.

She felt his hand on her other breast, his fingers

mimicking the actions of his mouth. A low moan escaped her as she slowly tipped her head backward, as the sensations doubled, as her throat grew tight, as her heart threatened to burst through her skin.

''Tell me to stop, Cassandra,'' she heard him say, his voice coming to her as if over a great distance. ''I'll stop, if that's what you want.''

She swallowed several times before she trusted herself to answer, could make her mouth form the words. ''Must I?''

His low-throated chuckle reverberated through her rib cage as he pressed his lips to the flatness of her midriff, as his hands slid down her outer thighs, then found their way back up that sensitive length, this time running beneath her skirt.

Slowly, still kissing her through her clothes, Sean eased himself onto his knees as she braced her hands on the edge of the countertop, praying she would be able to remain upright.

The light was on, even if Cassandra's eyes remained closed. The curtains were drawn back over the kitchen window, so that if nosy Mrs. Lyttle came into her kitchen next door to get herself a drink of water she was bound to be in for the surprise of her life.

And Cassandra didn't care. Couldn't care. She was much too busy realizing that the French cut of her panties did little to inhibit Sean's exploration of her belly, of the heated area between her legs.

He pushed her skirt upward, bunched the material in his hand, exposing her to the light, to his avid gaze. Such intimacy was shocking, and yet exciting, so that when Sean gently indicated that he wanted her to open her legs for him, open herself to him, she could only keep her eyes tightly closed and do as he indicated.

His hands molded her. His fingers learned her every secret. His lips branded her with hot, wet heat. And, just when she thought she couldn't stand on her shaky legs for another moment, sensation overwhelmed her.

She became boneless, floating even as she felt herself falling, only to be caught up in strong arms that lifted her, carried her.

Out of the kitchen. Down the hallway to the stairs. Up to her second-floor bedroom. To the stars, and beyond.

Moonlight spilled into the small room through three large windows, and Sean, his eyes at last adjusted to the dim moonlight as well as the illumination that came through the open door from the well-lit hallway, found it easy to focus on what interested him.

Cassandra's very private bedroom.

It was a virginal bedroom, the bedroom of a young girl rather than that of a woman, a career woman, an intensely passionate, loving woman.

The furniture was white, French provincial in style, with clusters of painted flowers marking the front of each drawer. The walls had been painted what looked to be a dusky pink, and were marked with small holes where posters of teenage heartthrobs had probably once been pinned.

His gaze traveled to the windows and to the sheer

white drapes, which some twist in his memory told him were Priscilla curtains. Now, how did he remember that? Oh, yeah. One of his foster mothers had hung Priscilla curtains in his bedroom the day before he'd been sent back to the home, telling him that *this* time she had requested a girl, as a female was bound to be less troublesome than a rowdy, uncontrollable boy of ten, who had dared to throw a baseball in her parlor and break her favorite lamp.

Sean decided he didn't like Cassandra's Priscilla curtains.

He rubbed his hand lightly down Cassandra's bare arm, carefully pulling her closer into his embrace as she slept beside him, her hand curled on his chest, a single leg thrown over his.

He continued his visual inventory of the room, preferring that to a mental rehash of all he had done this evening, all they had done, and the reasons behind why they had done it.

There was a large, silver-framed color photograph on her dresser. He focused on that and the figures of three people standing stiffly beside a wilting lilac bush. A man of more than fifty stood to the left of the young girl who had to be Cassandra. He was wearing a tweed jacket with suede patches on the elbows, and he held a pipe in the hand he had draped over the young Cassandra's shoulder.

Beside him, also with a hand on Cassandra's shoulder—What were they afraid of? That she'd run away if they didn't hold her down?—stood a woman who looked every day as old as her husband, and twice as reserved. Her mouth was drawn into a tight line of disapproval as she stared into the camera lens, her entire posture one of anxiousness to be done with this silliness so that she could be back at work, or wherever she really wanted to be—because she certainly did not look happy to be posing with her family.

Which was a pity, because Cassandra looked to be wearing the sort of dress girls wore to make their First Communion, or to be confirmed. In other words, the day the picture had been taken had been an important one in the young Cassandra's life. Important enough for her to keep the photograph on her dresser all these years.

Maybe it was the only family photograph she had? If Cassandra hadn't known how to rope and hog-tie her mother for another photograph, it most probably was.

Cassandra shifted slightly in her sleep, and Sean dropped a kiss on her hair as he closed his eyes and thought about the furnishings in the remainder of the house. Spare. Utilitarian. Drab. Useful, but not at all decorative. The walls in every room crowded with bookshelves.

He'd already figured out that this must be her parents' house, inherited by Cassandra after their deaths. But she had barely changed a thing since then. How long had they been dead? About five years? How long did it take for someone to put their own "stamp" on a house?

And why hadn't Cassandra bothered to do so?

There was a fairly new television set in the living room, and the office behind the kitchen was equipped with a new-looking computer and a sophisticated stereo system, but those were the only additions to the house that he felt confident had been Cassandra's idea.

The dark, overstuffed couches, the faded carpets, the heavy dining room furniture that wasn't antique but just *old,* were certainly not to her taste. At least, Sean didn't think so.

Just as he didn't think this "little girl" bedroom would ever have appealed to Cassandra, who was definitely not the frilly sort—except when it came to her absolutely marvelous underwear, he decided with a smile.

How little he knew about Cassandra Mercer. And how varied that information was. He knew her thoughts on education, and he knew that she had an interestingly sensitive spot behind her left knee. She liked the hot throb and heavy beat of contemporary music, but she didn't drink beer or alcohol. She wanted comfort in her car, but had a practical side that wouldn't let her be led to pay too much for that comfort.

And she haunted his dreams, waking and sleeping. Her smile could turn him inside-out. Her intelligent mouth could move him to anger, to laughter, to bed.

A bed he'd better soon leave, he remembered reluctantly, or else he wouldn't be home before Jason, which could prove awkward for both Cassandra and himself.

"Cassandra?" he whispered against her ear, smiling as she screwed up her face, then buried it deeper against his shoulder. "Cassandra, it's after midnight.

You have to take me home before I turn back into a pumpkin.''

''Uh-uh. Don't want to,'' she mumbled, wrapping her long limbs around him and nearly undermining his resolve. He had carried her upstairs and made love to her for more than two hours. Teaching her, learning about her, memorizing every inch of her, every soft, mewling sound she made when he touched her, as she touched him. Just the thought of that lovemaking made him want to do it all again. And this time he'd *really* take his time about the thing!

''Cassandra,'' he said, trying again, wishing he didn't have to be so damn responsible. ''Do you want me to call for a cab?''

''Will you use the phone—or just whistle?'' she asked, raising her head at last, pushing a hand through her hair to move its length away from her sleepy, smiling face.

''Just when I think I'm getting a handle on who you are…'' he began, then gave it up and kissed her, instead. That single kiss led to another, and then another, and the ticking clock on the nightstand was soon as forgettable as his thoughts about Cassandra's odd house.

But there was one thing he couldn't forget. He couldn't forget that, although he had prepared himself for a night spent making love to Cassandra, he had seriously underestimated her effect on him, and his own rather remarkable recuperative powers when faced with that effect.

''We can't,'' he mumbled against her mouth, even as she slid her hand low on his belly, turning his gut into a solid rock of longing. "You might have done better if I'd ever been a Boy Scout, if I remember one of their slogans correctly. Be Prepared, wasn't it?"

"Ummm," she mumbled, biting at his bottom lip, another trick he had taught her. God, but she was a fast learner! "And they're trustworthy, too. Like Jeeps. But that's another argument, isn't it? Do you really have to leave?"

"'Fraid so, sweetheart," he answered, turning on the light on the nightstand and throwing back the thin sheet that was all that covered them, then laughing as she pulled it back up to her chin—just as if he hadn't already seen, touched and tasted all of her.

"And you're leaving for Vail in the morning," Cassandra said, thrilling him with her willingness to allow him to hear the disappointment in her voice.

He leaned across the bed and kissed her once more, briefly, before she could raise her arms and pull him back down to her. "Nope. My responsible son has a job, as he reminded me. But that doesn't mean I'm giving up the first vacation I've taken in years. So, you want to do something tomorrow, Cassandra? Take a drive, go for a walk—make love until we both go cross-eyed?"

Her grin was youthful, but colored by a new maturity, a new sense of feminine power, he believed. "If I pick door number three, would you consider me forward? Pushy? Hoydenish?"

"Hoydenish?" Sean repeated, laughing. "Where did you come up with that one?"

"I've been reading Jane Austen," she told him as

she sat up, wrapping herself in the sheet as she levered her legs over the edge of the bed. ''Very educational books, actually. I'm thinking of making a few of them assignments for Jason. He enjoys surfing the Internet for research papers entirely too much for it to be considered any sort of punishment.''

''And reading Jane Austen would be a punishment?''

She stood up, slinging the edge of the sheet over her shoulder, so that she appeared to be wearing a very sexy toga. ''No, not at all. But the book reports I'll insist on will probably kill him,'' she said with a smile, then frowned as the phone rang. ''Do you think Jason's checking up on us?'' she asked as she reached for the receiver. ''Hello…Jason? Jason—what's wrong?''

Sean finished buttoning his slacks and reached for the receiver, all in one motion. ''Jase? Is there a problem?''

He listened for a few moments, watching Cassandra as his son spoke, then said, ''Stay where you are. We'll be right there,'' and handed her the phone. ''Get dressed, Cassandra. Jason and Becky were in an accident.''

''Are—are they hurt? Was he calling from the hospital?'' Her earlier modesty cast aside with the sheet, she grabbed her clothing from the floor, where it had landed in a heap more than three hours ago, and struggled to get dressed. ''Sean? Are you going to answer me?''

''Jason says he's all right,'' he said, rubbing his fingers over his cheek, rubbing the palm of his hand across his chin. "They're examining Becky in the emergency room now. Damn it! Why did I let him have the Mercedes? I should have known he'd have to go showing off, speeding! Where are your keys? In the kitchen? Finish dressing, Cassandra. I'll meet you at the car."

She ran after him, holding her shoes under her arm as she buttoned a fresh blouse she had pulled from the closet. "Did Jason tell you the accident was his fault?"

"He didn't have to," Sean flung over his shoulder at her as he ran down the steps. "All he had to tell me was that the police were with him and waiting to talk to me."

"Well," Cassandra said as she skidded around the corner of the hallway, "that doesn't prove anything. You're jumping to conclusions again, Sean. Thinking the worst before you even know anything. Over—"

Sean stopped dead at the entrance to the kitchen, so that Cassandra barreled into his chest as he turned around to face her. "*Overreacting,* Cassandra? Is that what you were going to say?"

"Sean—"

"No!" he exclaimed, holding up his hands to stop her from defending his son. "Not this time, Cassandra. It's always two steps forward and one step back with that kid. Give him an inch and he takes a mile. Offer your hand and he grabs for the whole arm. You name the cliché, and Jase will live up to it. Just like his mother, just like me! Or did you forget that we just climbed out of your bed? Without a word of love, a syllable of promise, a mention of commitment—I took all you offered, all I could take, all I could make you give. And then some!''

"You didn't *make* me give anything I didn't want to give,'' Cassandra said quietly, her soft brown eyes glittering with tears. "Nobody and nothing has control over my life, my actions. Not anymore. Not ever again. Now, are we going to stand here so I can listen to you being stupid, or are we going to the hospital to see about Jason and Becky?''

"God, what an ass I am! My kid's in the hospital and all I'm doing is feeling sorry for myself.'' He put his hands on her shoulders. "I don't know why you just don't tell me to go to hell.''

"I don't know why, either,'' she said, turning her head to press a kiss against the back of his hand. "But I think you have potential. Now, come on, Jason needs you. I'll drive.''

Fifteen

Cassandra drove through the dark night, heading toward Vanderbilt Memorial, a disturbingly intense and quiet Sean in the front passenger seat. It had begun to rain, and the only sound inside the car was the soft *swish-swish* of the windshield wipers—and the beating of Cassandra's heart.

She could feel Sean's fear, his anxiety, his need to be with his son. She also sensed his anger at himself for believing Jason to have been at fault when, as she had pointed out, no one yet knew what had happened.

As if reading her thoughts, Sean said quietly, "He said he was all right. But what's all right? I remember a friend of mine, from college. He was injured in a sledding accident one winter, but swore he was fine. And he looked fine. He got up, he walked around, he talked. And then, about ten minutes later, he just fell down. He—he was dead by the time the paramedics arrived. Internal bleeding, they told us later. Cassandra, if anything were to happen to Jason, I—"

"Jason said he was fine, so he's fine," she told him quickly, reaching across the small space that divided them, the chasm that divided her from his parental pain. "We'll be there in ten minutes, all right? Damn, hasn't it rained enough in this past week?"

"Do you want to pull over, let me drive?"

Cassandra shook her head, looking out onto the rain-bright street, the reflection of the streetlights on the macadam. "I can manage. Oh—look up there, ahead of us, to those blinking lights. Do you think—?"

"Pull over behind that cruiser, Cassandra," Sean said, both his hands braced on the dashboard. "That's my car they're loading onto the flatbed tow truck."

Cassandra, her lips caught between her teeth, did as Sean asked, pulling the car to a stop behind a shiny white police car whose red, white and blue lights were still blinking out their warning, streaking the rainy night with color, with a sense of urgency that sent a sickening knot to tighten in the pit of her stomach.

They were both out of the car and running toward the tow truck before any of the policemen or firemen who were on the scene could stop them, Sean calling out who he was and that he was the owner of the Mercedes.

Or what used to be a Mercedes, Cassandra thought as she stopped in her tracks, looking at the car in horror. There was barely anything left of the passenger side of the car. She walked forward more slowly, wiping raindrops from her face, squinting as she took off her wet glasses and taking in the sight of the deflated passenger-door air bag that had deployed when the car was hit.

The dashboard air bags hadn't deployed, which meant that the impact had all been from the side, and Cassandra looked around, hunting for the source of that impact. She counted up the three police cruisers, the single fire truck—with half a dozen firemen busy washing down the street with hoses they'd pulled from the pumper truck. Cassandra could smell gasoline fumes and looked at the street, seeing the oily rainbows of color that told her at least one of the vehicles involved in the accident had leaked gasoline from its fuel tank.

"Thank God there wasn't a fire," she said as one of the policemen approached her.

"You with Mr. Frame, ma'am?" the officer inquired, and Cassandra nodded.

"Where's the other car?" she then asked, wondering if it looked as bad as the Mercedes. If it did, there may have been more injuries, even a fatality.

"We're looking for it now, ma'am," the officer told her, motioning for her to step back. The tow truck was ready to move out, Sean's twisted car perched on the flatbed like some sort of horrible modern art. "It was a hit-and-run, according to the kid. And there's white paint on his rear bumper, so we believe him. Someone hit him from the rear, at least twice, and he went spinning out on the wet street. Ended up sliding against that light pole over there, at the entrance to the intersection. It was quite an impact, which happens when a car is thrown into a spin."

Sure enough, the light pole was leaning drunkenly over the street, something she hadn't noticed at first. The damage had all been to the Mercedes. The gas that had spilled on the street had been from the Mercedes.

Jason and Becky had been attacked! And they could have been killed!

"Somebody—somebody did this *deliberately?*"
Cassandra looked toward Sean and saw him striding
in her direction, the cold, concentrated look on his
face telling her that one of the other policemen had
already given him the information she'd just heard.
"My God. Why? Sean?"

He took hold of her outstretched hand. "Come on,
Cassandra, we're going to Vanderbilt to talk to Jason.
The officer told me he swears he didn't recognize the
other car, but I want to hear it from his own mouth,
while he's looking into my eyes. Into *your* eyes."

She ran to the driver's side of her car and slid inside, already turning the key in the ignition. "I don't
get it, Sean," she said as she carefully pulled around
the cruiser, avoiding the area where the firemen were
just finishing hosing down the street, then heading for
the hospital once more, this time with more than
worry and fear riding along with her. Now she was
also angry. Very, very angry!

Sean was sitting very still, staring straight ahead,
water droplets glistening in his hair, his face lit by
each streetlight they passed. His jaw was set tight, his
shoulders squared. He looked ready to take on the
world, and heaven help anyone who dared to get in
his way.

"What don't you get, Cassandra?" he asked tightly
as the lights of Vanderbilt Memorial at last appeared
in the distance. "That someone would deliberately
run someone else's car off the street? To some minds,
that's what's known as good, clean fun. And an in-
experienced young kid driving a luxury car? Hell, that
must have made it twice the fun!"

"So, you think that whoever did this was really after the car? Or, if I get this right, after the kid who they saw driving such a car? That doesn't make sense."

"It doesn't have to, Cassandra," he shot back tersely, then pointed toward the windshield. "Turn up there, just before that sign pointing out the emergency entrance. The officer said someone will meet us there."

She put on her turn signal, then began to slow down. She really didn't like driving at night, especially in the rain, especially when there were so many lights—lights that seemed to turn into bright star bursts as they shone through the windscreen at her, hurting her eyes.

"Are you saying this all happened because a bunch of kids were out joyriding and just happened to see Jason and Becky?" she asked, trying to understand. "That the reason the kids could be injured, your car totaled, the police and fire departments called out— this entire mess—is because a couple of bored kids felt like having a little *fun?*"

He shot her an intense look as she pulled into one of the specially marked parking spaces for those coming to the emergency room. "That's exactly what I'm saying, Cassandra. Now, can you tell me which of your students—your current kids, or any who graduated, or any who dropped out—you believe capable of considering damn near killing somebody else *fun?* Think about it, okay?"

She sat in the car, her hand on the ignition key, watching as Sean slammed the passenger door and began jogging toward the emergency room entrance. One of *her* kids? One of *her* students? Capable of such stupidity? Such dangerous horseplay? No. No, it couldn't be. Not one of *her* kids.

"Oh, God," she said, and slowly lowered her forehead on the steering wheel, feeling sick to her stomach.

Sean saw Jason immediately, and stopped himself before he could rush across the room to his son. Taking a deep breath and looking at him, Sean visually assessed him as if for damage. Jason looked completely normal, except for the grayish cast to his skin and the untidiness of his hair which, even as Sean watched, Jason rumpled with his fingers as he sighed audibly.

He looked scared, shaken and about twelve years old. Sean's heart constricted, and he had to take several more deep breaths before he could force his legs to move.

"Dad!" Jason exclaimed, his eyes shining with relief as he turned in his chair and saw Sean. He jumped up hurriedly, then sat down again, his quick smile gone, his gaze intent on the tile floor.

Sean knew what his son was thinking, what he feared. He believed that his father would be madder than hell and immediately start yelling at him. Which wouldn't have been far from wrong, Sean supposed, if he hadn't been with Cassandra when the news first came, and hadn't had her to yell at, to vent his anger to, when his fear turned to a stupid outburst of impotent fury.

But now he'd had time to think, time for the first jolt of fear to be overcome by reason. And it didn't matter that he'd already found out that the accident hadn't been his son's fault. Nothing mattered right now, damn it, except that his son was all right.

Sean quickly crossed the room, nodding to the uniformed officer who was propping up the wall beside Jason, and then dropped to his knees in front of the boy.

"Jase?" he asked quietly, laying a hand on the boy's knee. "Have the doctors checked you out? Are you sure you're all right?"

Jason nodded, still keeping his head down. "Dr. Howell checked me out a while ago. I'm just sore, where the seat belt grabbed at me, I guess. He gave me some muscle relaxant pills, or something like that. Becky's okay, too. She—she was pretty upset. Crying and stuff. Screaming. But she's okay. They're just going to keep her overnight because she might have hit her head or something. The police said the air bag probably saved her." He slowly raised his head, his eyes shining with tears. "I—I'm so sorry about the car, Dad. I know how much you loved it."

"The car," Sean said hollowly, feeling his bottom lip beginning to tremble, feeling the prickle of tears behind his eyes. "Jase, I don't give two damns about the car. Just as long as *you're* all right. Do you understand what I'm saying? I love you, son. I love you so much."

The next thing Sean knew, a sobbing Jason was draped against him, holding him so tightly he could feel each of his fingertips pressing into his back. "I love you, too, Dad,'' he gulped out against his father's neck as Sean returned his embrace, holding his son as the two of them knelt on the floor, rocking him in his arms, letting him cry.

After a few moments Sean felt a hand on his shoulder and looked up to see Cassandra standing beside him, tears running down her cheeks as she smiled down at him. He knew his own cheeks were wet, and he didn't care. All he cared about was that it seemed so right that Cassandra be here with him, with him and Jason. Now. When their world was upside-down. Because, thanks to Cassandra, maybe they had a chance to turn it upright once more.

''Sean?'' Cassandra inquired quietly. ''When you have a moment, this officer would like to speak with you and Jason. He has to take his statement and wanted you to be here because Jase is only seventeen. Do you think Jason is up to it, or should we ask if this can wait until tomorrow morning?''

Sean gave Jason a last hug, then helped him back into his chair and rose to his feet. ''What do you say, Jase? Are you ready to tell the officer what you know?''

Jason wiped at his eyes with the back of his hand, then accepted the box of tissues Cassandra had found somewhere and offered to him. He avoided looking directly at Cassandra, at the officer, at his father. ''There's not much to say, Dad.''

The policeman stepped forward, opening a notebook he'd been holding. ''My partner has already spoken with your friend Becky, Jason,'' he said kindly, ''and she doesn't remember much beyond a pair of headlights coming at the rear of the car a couple of times, the jolts, and then the squealing of the tires when you lost control of the vehicle. Maybe you can be of more help to us? We know the other vehicle was white, but that's all we know so far.''

''Jason?'' Sean prompted when his son still said nothing. ''Why was the driver after you? Had you cut him off or something? Upset him in some way?''

''I—I don't know,'' Jason said, then looked up at the officer. ''Maybe.'' He ran his tongue around his lips. ''Yeah. Maybe I did something to get him mad. White, huh? All I could see was headlights. Like Becky. You know, all those lights, and the rain and all? Can I please go home now?''

Sean looked at the officer, who was already closing his notebook. ''He's pretty shaken up, don't you think? I can bring him by the station tomorrow sometime, maybe in the afternoon? Around three, if that's all right? By then he might have remembered something else.''

''Yeah, that'll be all right,'' the officer said, then put a hand on Jason's shoulder. ''Look, son, I know how it is. You don't want to squeal on anybody, right? You might even think they'll get off with a slap on the wrist and then come after you, right? Well, think about this, too. That little girl in there might have been killed tonight. You might have been killed. My partner and I, instead of standing here taking notes, might have been knocking on two doors, telling two sets of parents that their kids were smeared all over the street.''

Jason looked at his father. ''But I didn't see anything. Honest.''

''And this isn't the first time this has happened, Jason,'' the officer continued, just as if Jason hadn't spoken, hadn't denied any knowledge of who had run him down, caused his accident. ''We've had two similar incidents in the past year, although this is the first time we've gotten so much as the white paint we found on the back of your dad's car to give us something to go on. Son, you have to help us if you can. Help us now, before somebody else's kids get killed.''

''I—I don't remember anything,'' Jason repeated, and Sean could see the fear in his son's eyes, hear it in his voice. ''Honest, Dad. Why won't anyone believe me? I didn't see anything but the lights! I just want to go home, okay? I want to go home!''

Cassandra gave out a small cry and pulled the weeping Jason to his feet, gathering him close as she walked him toward the door, hesitating only long enough to throw the officer, and Sean, a withering look over her shoulder. Clearly she felt that Jason had had enough for one night, and that it was time to take him home, feed him some warm milk and put him to bed.

''I'll have him at the station tomorrow at three, officer,'' Sean said, shaking the man's hand. ''And, I promise you, he'll be a lot more cooperative then.''

''Good enough, sir,'' the officer told him, reaching for his helmet and gloves, for he was clearly a motorcycle officer. ''I gotta get back out there on my bike, anyway. Just let your wife baby him for a while, fuss over him the way women do, and then we'll give it another try. He's scared now, confused, but he knows something. I'd bet my badge on it.''

Sean opened his mouth to tell the officer that Cassandra wasn't his wife, or Jason's mother. She was, of all things, his son's guidance counselor. And a namby-pamby guidance counselor at that, whose methods he disagreed with, whose "all kids are good kids" theories made his teeth ache. But he didn't bother explaining, because it didn't matter. Not really.

Did it?

No. No, it didn't. Because Jason needed her. *He* needed her.

And they all needed to hear the truth.

Cassandra sat on the living room floor, a half dozen Burke Senior High School yearbooks spread out around her, a notepad on her knee as she gnawed on the end of a pencil. Absently, she scratched Festus behind his left ear as the cat rolled onto his back in ecstasy.

There was something more than a little distasteful to her about thumbing through page after page of photographs of smiling young teens, looking for anyone who looked capable of running a car off the road and endangering two other young lives.

But Jason knew something. Much as she'd like to deny it, she had seen it in his eyes. Seen the terrible knowledge there. Seen the fear. And she was certain his father had seen it, as well.

Thank God he hadn't pushed at Jason last night. He'd told her to take Jason to the car while he went to speak for a moment to Becky's parents before the girl was moved upstairs to a room. The ride back to the Frame house was long and silent. Sean had then handed Jason the key to the house and told him to go upstairs and take a long, hot shower so that his muscles didn't stiffen up too much.

Only after Jason had opened the front door and gone inside did Sean say anything to her, tersely asking her to try to concentrate on the roster of Burke students, considering the possibility that any of them could be responsible for Jason's accident.

She'd agreed without argument, because she hadn't wanted to argue with him at that particular moment, and because he was probably right. There weren't many bad apples at Burke, but there had been a few over the years. She'd have to be a starry-eyed optimist not to know that.

But it still hurt. It still made her feel like a failure, because these teens had slipped through the cracks in the system, had gone bad even after all her efforts, all the efforts of the faculty and administration at Burke.

She picked up the hot-off-the-presses yearbook from the year just past and turned to page seventy-eight again, once more looking at the photographs that showed the junior class standing in a group on the steps of the school. A photograph of the girls. Another, on the facing page, featuring the boys.

Jason's class.

Jason was in the last row, his features scrunched up as he squinted into the bright sun, his hair a good four inches shorter than it was now, his neat clothing definitely more out of place than the T-shirts and jeans he now wore. How much younger he looked in the photograph! A single school year meant so much when you were sixteen, seventeen, heading for eighteen. Each year was a minilifetime.

Sighing, hating herself, she guided her fingertip along the rows of smiling faces, stopping once or twice to connect a face with the list of names beneath the photograph. Good kids. Such good kids. Oh, sure, they had their problems, their moments of rebellion, but they were basically good kids. All eighty-seven boys, all ninety-two girls.

Her kids.

She closed the book. She couldn't do this. Just couldn't. After all, she wasn't picking out mug shots or a possible criminal out of a lineup. These were smiling, happy teenagers.

But Sean would expect her to have come up with a list of names. The police might even expect it of her.

"Oh, Jason, just tell them the truth," she said out loud, remembering the look on his face last night as he had pleaded innocent to recognizing who had bumped into his car. And run him off the road. The boy had positively oozed guilt. And fear. Why, he was even ready to accept responsibility for the accident, all but leaping at the idea he could have done something to anger the other driver.

Just as he had not defended himself over the broken windows in the gymnasium, had been so willing to take the blame upon himself!

"But why?" she asked Festus, who was now pushing his head against her thigh. "Why would he do that?"

She stood up and walked to the door, to let Festus outside. She opened it to see Sean standing there, his hand raised and ready to ring the bell. "Sean!" she exclaimed, feeling a rush of color heating her cheeks, her memories of what had transpired between them last night, in her bedroom, coming back in full force.

"May I come in?" he asked, and she nodded, stepping back to allow him to walk past her, into the living room. He looked tired, exhausted, and as if he was in some pain.

"Would you like some coffee?" she asked as he stood in the middle of the room, looking down at the scattering of yearbooks. "Some lunch? I've got some leftover roast beef in the kitchen. It wouldn't take me a minute to—"

"Did you see any suspicious-looking characters in any of these?" he asked, cutting her off. "You know, someone who looks as shifty-eyed as Jason does when I ask him to tell me what happened last night."

Cassandra winced. "He's still not talking, huh?"

"Not talking, not shouting, not doing much of anything—except shaking his head and saying he really can't say anything, doesn't know anything. I don't think he slept at all last night. He hasn't had anything to eat so far today." Sean turned to look at her, his eyes dark with frustration. "He's afraid, Cassandra. My son is afraid, and he believes I can't protect him."

"Maybe he believes he's protecting *you,* Sean," Cassandra offered, not stopping to consider why she'd think, let alone say, such a thing.

Sean bent down and picked up one of the year-books. "Protecting *me?*" he repeated as he opened the book and began paging through it. "From what, Cassandra?"

She shrugged, taking in his defensive stance, his barely concealed anger. "From taking the law into your own hands? From protecting your son by going after these kids and doling out a little Wild West justice? I don't know, Sean—how can I know what Jason is thinking? But I do know that I'm going to make some lunch. Don't offer to help, though, because I don't think I'd want to see you anywhere near the knives. Not with that look on your face!"

She turned to leave the room, but Sean caught at her arm, pulling her around to face him. "I'm sorry, Cassandra," he said, leaning forward to kiss her cheek. "I have no business messing up your life with my problems, or with Jason's. I just know that I wouldn't want to go through this without you."

"Don't make me cry, Sean," she warned, leaning against his chest, his strength, his willingness to admit his own weaknesses. "That's not playing fair."

He heard his soft chuckle as he pressed his cheek against the top of her head. "Fair, Cassandra? Didn't you know that nothing's fair about either love or war?"

She lifted her head, looking up into his face. His wonderful, adorable face. "Are we loving or warring?"

"A little of both, I suppose," he said, taking her arm and leading her toward the kitchen. "However, once this business with Jason is settled, I think we'll try to concentrate on the love part of it, if that's all right with you? We've already had two years of practice on how to fight with each other.''

Cassandra shrugged free of his loose embrace and walked to the refrigerator to take out the leftover roast beef and a jar of mayonnaise. ''Has Jason said anything to you about us, Sean?'' she asked as she opened the bread drawer and lifted out a fresh bag of rolls. ''I mean, he certainly knew where to reach you last night, didn't he? I'm worried about that, as you've said you believe he has some sort of crush on me.''

Sean stepped past her, to pull two plates from the cabinet beside the sink. ''I shouldn't tell you this,'' he said, kissing her cheek again as she returned to the table, ''but Jase did say something to me last night.''

''Oh?'' Cassandra looked blindly out the window, wondering if she wanted to hear what Sean had to say.

''Yes, *oh*,'' he said, and she closed her eyes in relief, hearing the amusement in Sean's voice. ''He said he thought the whole thing was pretty cool once he'd gotten to thinking about it seriously. Then he started telling me the story of Damocles and the lion.''

Cassandra turned around to face him, her eyes wide. ''He told you *what?*''

Sean took two napkins from the holder on the center of the table, folded them and laid them beside the plates. ''You heard me. I was the lion, I believe, leaving you for the role of Damocles. You took the thorn from my paw, and I'm to reward you by not eating you next time I'm angry. In other words, Jason seems to think you have some sort of softening influence on me. He likes that. He likes that you were at the hospital last night. And I think—if I'm not too dense to live, as he would say—that we just got his blessing.''

··"How—how, um, how *nice*,'' Cassandra stammered, nearly slicing off her thumb as she drew the knife blade through the roast beef. She had Jason's blessing? For what? For love? For marriage? Or for a roll in the hay, if that was what it was still called. Because she sure hadn't heard any words of love from Sean—except now, when he was obviously joking with her. "Do—do you want mayonnaise?''

"That depends,'' Sean said from only inches behind her, somehow having come around the table to stand so close that she couldn't breathe, didn't want to breathe.

"It—it depends?''

"Um-hmm,'' he told her, his mouth hot against the side of her throat. "It depends on where you're planning to spread it, of course.''

She turned in his arms, smiling, feeling wonderfully sexy. "Hmm—I'd have to say that the possibilities are probably endless....''

They never did eat lunch before going to pick up Jason and take him to the police station.

Sixteen

Jason sat in the back seat of Sean's Blazer as all three of them drove toward the Grand Springs Police Station, the only sounds coming from the traffic outside and the radio playing in the dashboard.

"That's nice, isn't it?" Cassandra commented as they listened to the hourly news update, to hear that the single mother who had given birth in a taxicab during the mud slides and blackout was going home. And the brave, resourceful taxi driver now had a baby boy named after him. "So many sad stories these past few days, and so many happy ones. Grand Springs has a lot of heroes."

"Including Jason," Sean said, turning to smile at his son. "If it hadn't been for his clearheadedness in notifying the authorities that I hadn't come home, and for that man who was able to tell the police where he'd seen your Jeep, we might not have been so lucky."

"I saw the man's picture in this morning's paper. Did you see it?"

Sean had, but he could also see what Cassandra was doing—talking to fill the silence, keeping Jason's mind occupied with something other than the interview facing him in a few minutes. "No. Tell me about it."

"Well, according to the story, the man must have had some sort of accident before we saw him. Do you remember, Sean, how confused he looked, how terribly *haunted* he looked?"

Sean smiled, shaking his head. "No. I just saw how muddy he was, and wondered why he'd want to try to walk out of that mess instead of staying with us in your Jeep. But if you want him to be haunted, then I'll say he looked haunted. Definitely."

Cassandra glared at him. "Thanks a bunch. Anyway, it turns out he has amnesia. That's why his picture is in the paper—in hopes that someone will recognize him."

Jason leaned forward, resting his forearms against the back of Cassandra's seat. "Wow, that's something else! He doesn't know who he is? I've read about that stuff, and it's really interesting. People like this guy can remember the capital of South Dakota, but they can't remember their own names."

"Pierre," Sean said, putting on the turn signal as they approached another intersection.

"Huh?" Jason leaned closer to his father. "Is that the guy's real name?"

"No, Jason," Cassandra responded, giggling. "Pierre is the capital of South Dakota, remember?"

Jason slumped back against the seat. "I knew that," he grumbled, shooting his father a dirty look that Sean intercepted in the rearview mirror.

"Of course you did, son," he told him, turning into the parking lot of the police station. "Now, do you think you can bring yourself to remember anything else?''

''Sean—'' Cassandra began warningly, and he winced, knowing he had said precisely the wrong thing.

''Sorry, Jase,'' he apologized as all three of them got out of the Blazer and walked up to the front door of the station. ''It's just that I think you know something you're not saying, that's all. After all, *you* don't have amnesia, do you?''

''Oh, that was subtle,'' Cassandra whispered as Jason took the stairs two at a time, entering the building ahead of them. ''Tell me, Mr. Frame, could I interest you in Burke's Advanced Placement Psychology course? We have a wonderful teacher. Or maybe you'd like to monitor the Social Graces course you fought against last year? You know, the one you sneeringly called a totally useless Miss Manners Does Burke. You might pick up a few pointers.''

Sean held up his hands in surrender. ''All right, all right, so I goofed. Again. But you brought up this amnesiac, and, well, it seemed a reasonable segue in to getting Jason to talk. Oh, hell!'' he said, shaking his head. ''I give up, Cassandra. Total surrender, to every last one of your ideas—and I'll never fight you again at the school board meetings. Sign me up for both courses.''

''And you wouldn't mind if I'd like to see that statement put in writing, Mr. Frame?'' she asked, smiling up at him. ''I'm sure I can get someone to give me a piece of paper—if you'd be willing to open a vein.''

God! What a bright, funny, wonderful woman had been hidden from him these past two years. And how mind-blowingly wonderful that he had found her at last! He would have kissed her then and there, with several of Grand Springs' finest looking on, except that the officer who had been in the emergency room last night stepped forward, asking them to accompany him to one of the offices, where Jason was already waiting.

With Sally.

"Sally?" he said before he could stop himself, which earned him one of her most condescending smiles as she crossed her long legs, then daintily tugged at the hem of her thigh-high skirt. She was blonder than he remembered her, but just as beautiful. The body that belied the fact that she'd had two children, the face that had launched a thousand love affairs and a pair of marriages in her thirty-five pampered years.

"Very good, Sean," she purred. "You remembered my name. I wouldn't have thought so, seeing as how I had to hear about our son's accident from strangers. And, before you ask, a reporter phoned me this morning, to verify a few facts before running a story about *my* son's accident. And who is this you have hiding behind you, darling—Little Miss Muppet?"

"That's Little Miss Muffet, Mom," Jason broke in, looking sheepish, and woefully embarrassed by his maternal parent, who was certainly in top form this afternoon. "The Muppets are puppets, at least, sort of. Muffets are...they're—well, anyway, they're different.''

Sally Taylor gave a dismissive wave of her left hand. The left hand with the rock on it the size of downtown Boulder. ''Whatever, darling. I'm sure it doesn't matter to me at all. Unless you're a lawyer here to represent my son, Ms.—''

''Mercer,'' Cassandra said, stepping forward, her right hand outstretched. ''Cassandra Mercer. I'm Jason's guidance counselor at Burke. And you must be Jason's mother. I'm very pleased to meet you.''

Sally looked at Sean, then back to Cassandra, pointedly ignoring her offer to shake hands. ''Oh, I seriously doubt that, Ms. Mercer. As a matter-of-fact, and I'm sure Jason will correct me if I'm misquoting, I'm probably your worst nightmare.'' She looked straight at Cassandra's modest blouse. ''After all, some comparisons can be so, shall we say, *deflating?*''

''Sally,'' Sean began, stepping forward, ''I don't think this is either the time or the place for a performance of one of your less appealing one-act plays. Now, if we could just—''

''I'm taking him back home with me, Sean,'' Sally declared, her smile replaced by a mouth-curling grin that reminded him of the Grinch when he announced he was about to steal Christmas. ''Where he belongs. I've already discussed it with Bob, and he agrees. We're going to enroll him in the same military school Bob attended. It's in Pennsylvania, I believe. Very historic—named after a battlefield or something. It's about time Jason learned a little something about discipline. That *was* what you said to me before you brought him here and then handed him the key to a sixty-thousand-dollar automobile and told him to go play, wasn't it?''

"I—I'll wait outside," Cassandra said, already backing toward the door.

"No, don't!" Jason all but shouted, leaping to his feet. "Please don't go, Ms. Mercer. I'd really like you to stay." He turned to the plainclothes officer who was seated behind a desk, doodling on a pad. "Detective Canfield, would that be okay with you?"

"Well, really, Jason, darling," Sally protested, smoothing down her skirt once more. "There's no need for histrionics, I'm sure. Now, why don't we just get on with it. We have to go back to your father's house and pack up your clothing. Not that it's good for anything but rags. Is there actually some sort of *purpose* behind having those holes in the knees of your pants? Sean, I'm surprised you allow this.''

"Dad?" Jason looked at Sean, obviously appealing for his help.

"Let's just get through the interview for now, Jason," he told his son. "We'll discuss family matters later, outside." He longed to tell Jason that he wasn't going anywhere, that Sally could threaten and bluster all she wanted and it meant nothing, because *he* had the court order granting him permanent custody of his son. The custody arrangement she had been only too happy to make less than a year ago. But that would only set his ex-wife off again.

Sally was only out to make as much trouble as she could, because Sally liked to make trouble. She reveled in it. She liked an audience, and she demanded that she have her share of adoring fans, even if she had to buy their favor. As she had done with Jason. As she had done with her husband, Bob, who had taken Jason's place as her number one fan, so that she had discarded her son as someone else would throw away yesterday's newspaper or a toy that no longer appealed.

What a lousy mess! But the action prompted by the hormones of an eighteen-year-old in the back seat of a '68 Malibu should never be held against the older and wiser thirty-five year old who was doing his damnedest to make right a long-ago mistake. That's what Sean thought. Not held against his hormones, nor against Sally's.

They had made a mistake, the pair of them. A big one. Granted. But they had lucked out with Jason, who was no sort of punishment, but a gift from God, a responsibility, a joy, a lifetime commitment who deserved everything good his parents could provide.

He didn't deserve to be turned into a tennis ball, batted back and forth between his parents—who were only trying to hurt each other for that long-ago immature explosion of hormones that had changed their lives forever.

"Detective Canfield?" Sean asked, going over to shake the officer's hand. "Is it all right with you if Mrs. Taylor and Ms. Mercer and I remain?"

The detective nodded. "You don't have to worry, Mr. Frame. This is a question-and-answer sort of thing, not a formal interrogation. You don't need a lawyer for young Jason or anything like that. He's a witness, a victim. He's not being charged with a crime."

"I think perhaps we should rethink this and have a lawyer present, Sean," Sally interrupted, leaning across the desk at Detective Canfield, giving him a good glimpse of her quite generous endowments. "Perhaps I should call George, Dad's attorney? He can be here in two hours."

"To do what, Sally?" Sean asked, feeling his temper rising. "Rewrite Jason's trust fund? George Livingstone isn't a criminal attorney, he's a two-hundred-dollar-an-hour wing-tipped corporate lawyer, remember?"

Cassandra cleared her throat delicately, stepping between the seated Sally and Sean, turning herself into some sort of football blocker—or offering herself as a human sacrifice. "Jason, perhaps it would be easier for you if we *all* waited outside?"

Detective Canfield stood as Jason nodded, averting his eyes from both his parents. "If you don't mind, sir, ladies? Honestly, this will only take a couple of minutes. If Jason knows as little as young Becky does, we're probably just indulging in a little wishful thinking here in the first place. But we have to try."

"Please, Dad? Mom?" Jason looked ready to cry, which couldn't be good for him, not when he had arrived at the police station already a bundle of nerves. "I really want to get this over with, you know? And if you and Mom are going to keep arguing—"

"You got it, Jase," Sean said, taking Sally's elbow

and squeezing it tightly as she began to protest. "We're going to wait outside, Sally. All of us."

"I always hated you most when you decided to be masterful," his ex-wife said, but she got to her feet anyway, and Cassandra opened the glass-topped door, allowing Sean and Sally to exit the room ahead of her, then following at what Sean believed her to naively think might be a safe distance.

Sally Taylor was beautiful. No doubt about it. Cassandra could see where Jason had gotten his fine bone structure, his natural grace of movement.

She could also see where Jason had "gotten" some of his problems. Sean and Sally were like oil and water. Or gasoline and a match. They couldn't seem to be in a room together for more than a moment before striking sparks off each other—with Jason in the middle, getting burned.

Marriage wasn't for everyone. Neither, it seemed, was divorce. Separate cities, separate countries, separate *planets* might not be enough to stop the seventeen-year war the two of them had obviously declared on each other. Sally seemed to be the one who went on the offensive first in any battle, and she didn't appear to be the type who took any prisoners.

Which meant that Cassandra was being sized up as a possible opponent, and already penciled-in as Sally Taylor's next victory.

Well, Cassandra wasn't about to raise the white flag just yet, thank you. Not when her love for Sean, for Jason, had sent her blood pressure soaring. Not that she would go looking for a fight, but she wouldn't back away from one, either. Although, she'd rather use reason and Sally's motherly instincts—she had to have some, didn't she?—to help Jason. To help Sean.

While Sean, at Cassandra's request, reluctantly went off to find the coffee machine, Sally sat down on one of the straight-back wooden chairs in the main area of the police station, crossed those lovely long legs and looked up at Cassandra.

"He's a fairly competent lover, don't you think? Not terribly inventive, but competent."

As opening shots went, this one whizzed straight across the bow, signaling a full assault was soon to come, if Cassandra didn't do something to stop it right now. Denying that she and Sean had become lovers seemed pointless, juvenile and futile.

Sally Taylor was one of those women who somehow instinctively sensed the relationship between a man and woman and just how involved that relationship might be. This "ability" constantly surprised Cassandra, who still had difficulty believing her own parents had ever had sex. Really, she probably was miles too naive to even think about going head-to-head with Sally Taylor, but she was going to give it her best shot.

"Oh, I don't know," Cassandra said as she sat down on the backless wooden bench that was jammed up against the wall. "As I was saying to Sean just the other night, as we were swinging from those chandeliers…" She let her voice drop off as she smiled, and waited for whatever would come next.

"Very funny, Ms. Mercer," Sally said after a moment, looking at Cassandra more carefully, reassessing her adversary. "You're not at all his type, you know. When he looks up from his work, which isn't often, he is usually more drawn to looks than brains, my dear. And where *did* you get that horrible dress? It must be at least three sizes too large. Surgical embellishment is a much more effective measure than camouflage, you know. I can recommend a wonderful plastic surgeon in Denver, if you're interested. Although he is pricey. Probably way above your reach. You teach, is that right?"

Cassandra was becoming bored. Sally Taylor had insulted her enough, from her appearance, her taste, her occupation, to her pocketbook. And all in the space of a few sentences. "As I've already mentioned, I'm a guidance counselor," she corrected her. "I listen and I learn. One of the things I've learned is a saying some of my students seem to use on one another to great advantage, although its meaning does escape me. Perhaps you'll know it?" She leaned forward slightly and said quietly, satisfyingly, "Bite me, Mrs. Taylor."

The woman sat there, beautiful and speechless.

"Now," Cassandra went on quickly, "if we have all that out of the way, perhaps you might want to discuss Jason. He is why you drove all the way over here, isn't he?"

Sally opened her Gucci bag and drew out a gold cigarette case, then grimaced as she looked up at the No Smoking signs that were plastered on all the walls. She sighed, put the cigarette case away and said amicably enough, "It's probably not wise to break the law *inside* the police station, I suppose. Very well,

Ms. Mercer—Cassandra—I apologize for sniping. It's just that Sean has always been capable of bringing out the bitch in me, just by being in the same room. I *am* interested in Jason. He is, after all, my son. Something his father conveniently forgets," she ended bitterly, obviously finding it difficult to string more than two sentences together without throwing an insult in her ex-husband's direction.

Cassandra folded her hands in her lap, eager to get down to cases. "Tell me a little bit about Jason, would you? Was he a quiet child? Did he have many friends? Why do you think he began rebelling last year?"

"Rebelling? Is that what you call it?"

"Rebelling, acting-out," Cassandra said, nodding. "Growing up might be another way of saying it. Sometimes we're too quick to put labels on children. I don't want to do that. But I think Jason is having a difficult time learning who he is. Being a teenager is difficult no matter what the family circumstances, but a child of divorce has even more challenges to face."

Sally opened her purse once more, brought out the cigarette case and began to stroke it, as if it might soothe her in some way. "I failed Jason. I failed him badly," she said softly, so that Cassandra had to lean closer in order to hear the woman above the din in the room now that two policemen were bringing in a struggling, wild-eyed, disheveled-looking man who seemed to be high on either drugs or alcohol. "Oh, God—what an awful place this is! I can't believe Jason is here. I just can't!"

Cassandra waved Sean away as he approached

them carrying a cardboard tray containing three large paper cups filled with steaming coffee. ''Come on, Mrs. Taylor,'' she said gently to Sally, taking her arm and guiding her toward the door. ''You can smoke outside.''

They found a bench under a tree and sat down, Cassandra waiting until Sally lit her cigarette, took a deep drag, blew out the smoke in a long, thin blue stream, then sighed. ''God, how I wish I didn't need this, but I do. I quit while I was pregnant with Jesse, then started up again when Jason began giving us trouble. It's an addiction, you know, and I dare anyone to call it nothing more than a bad habit! Someday, if the zealots have their way, they'll be dragging me off to a jail cell for lighting up in my own house, like that man we just saw in there. I only hope my cell is next to one of the manufacturers of these cancer sticks.''

Cassandra didn't say anything, because there was nothing to say in answer to that statement. She just sat there, waiting, knowing that Sally would say what she had to say in her own good time. It was enough that they weren't sparring, that Sally seemed to be beginning to trust her. If she wanted to listen to the birds for a while, watch the cars driving by, that was fine with Cassandra. She could wait.

''I never loved Sean,'' Sally Taylor said at last, her statement shocking Cassandra, so that she could only blink, then listen. ''He was dangerous, you know? Not at all like any of my friends, anybody I grew up with. Different. No money, no station, but popular as all hell and damn handsome—or as handsome as a seventeen-year-old can be. The football captain and the head of the cheerleader squad. The teenage equivalent of Kismet, I suppose.''

She took another drag on her cigarette. ''Being a mother is very sobering, very scary. I dread thinking about what's facing Jason out there today, what will face Jesse tomorrow. Thank God for today's sex education classes, I suppose. We sure could have used them.''

Cassandra smiled. ''Would you be willing to move to Grand Springs and run for the school board?'' she asked, shaking her head. ''I think I could use your forthrightness to convince some of those guys that teenagers have been experimenting with sex for a long time, and that it's not a destructive new invention of television or movies or even politicians. I'm sorry, I've interrupted you, but you've hit on something that's near and dear to my heart since I got my degree. You were saying?''

''If you think you're worried now, wait until you have a couple of kids of your own. This blond hair covers up more than a few gray roots, you know.'' Sally blew out a stream of smoke, from her nostrils this time. She really was a perfect advertisement for the tobacco industry. Beautiful, healthy-looking, successful. On her, smoking looked good. Sexy. Not at all deadly.

''I was thrilled to be pregnant,'' she said after a moment. ''I thought it would mean I didn't have to go to college, like Daddy wanted. All I saw was the rosy picture, you know? But it wasn't like that. Not at all. So I ran away. From Sean, from Jason.'' She grinned at Cassandra. "And I had a hell of a good time, for a lot of years."

"Leaving Jason with your parents?"

She shrugged. "With whoever. I treated him like a toy, just as Sean says. Which was all right when he was cute and cuddly. But then he grew into that most horrible of creatures—a teenager. I didn't know what to do with him, so I bought him off. Gave him anything he wanted, which was easy, because he was basically a good kid. Good grades, well behaved. Until I got married again and Jesse was born. I suppose Sean has told you that, as well?"

"He did say you spoiled Jason, yes." Cassandra was beginning to feel uncomfortable. She had been prepared to dislike Sally Taylor, and she couldn't agree with the way the woman had lived her life. And yet, there was something vulnerable about her, something sad.

"I love Bob," Sally said, tossing the cigarette to the ground and grinding it out with the toe of her stylish shoe. "Sean was the wrong man at the wrong time. Bob was the right one. And Jesse was wanted by both of us." She turned to look at Cassandra. "With Jesse, I might not do everything right, but I'm giving it my best shot, you know? I'm a good mother now, even if I'm coming to it a little late. A *lot* late. I'd have sixty fits if anyone treated that child the way I treated Jason. Spoiling him, ruining him, neglecting him. That's why I let Sean have him. To make up for all the years I kept them apart."

"You kept Sean away from Jason?"

"You could say that. The Christmas holidays in

Switzerland, the summer vacations in Daddy's beach house in the Bahamas. Sean protested, but he was busy building his empire—making my Daddy quite a wealthy man in the bargain. I hated Sean for that, too, in case you're wondering. Everything he touched seemed to turn to gold. If I could find a way to make him unhappy, I used it. Jason was...*handy*.''

She reached for another cigarette, then seemed to change her mind. ''Sean's too hard on him, isn't he?'' she asked, touching Cassandra's forearm. ''He expects him to be perfect, like he is. And now Jason is involved with the police! I don't really intend to send him to military school—just said that to tweak at Sean.''

She blew out her breath in exasperation, her shoulders slumping. ''Which only hurt Jason, didn't it? Oh, what a mess we've made of that sweet boy!''

Cassandra moved to the edge of the bench, hardly able to contain herself. ''But you're wrong! Jason is a wonderful boy. Bright, intelligent, *kind*—one of the sweetest kids I've ever met! He's in some sort of trouble right now, I agree, but he was really making strides this past year, especially since Christmas, when he began to find his niche. He's got wonderful friends, he's trying out for place kicker on the football squad this fall, he's anxious to go to college. If you and Sean would stop seeing your own failings in him, looking for faults he might have inherited or whatever, maybe you'd see that.''

''She's right, Sally,'' Sean said, and Cassandra nearly jumped out of her skin, not having realized that he had come up to them and overheard what she'd said. "Jason is a good kid. I might regret a lot that I've done in my life, but I'll never regret having Jason. And, if I haven't thanked you for having him, for letting me take him this past year, I want to thank you now."

"Thank me? Are we calling a truce, Sean? Why, yes, I believe we are." Sally blinked her beautiful blue eyes several times, as if fighting back tears, then stood up, giving Sean a kiss on the cheek. "We've been a fine pair of fools, haven't we, Sean? Is Jason finished in there yet? I—I think I'd like to take him out for ice cream or something before I bring him home to you. I want him to visit me, but we'll plan something for later this summer, once you two are more settled. All right?"

Sean looked toward the entrance to the police station. "Jason's just coming out now. You go on, Sally, and I'll meet you later, at home." He slipped his arm around Cassandra's back. "Right now, I think I want to tell this woman how crazy I am about her."

"Smooth, Sean," Sally said, smiling at Cassandra. "You always were smooth. And so damn lucky. I'll see you later." She walked away from them, beautiful, elegant and more human than Cassandra would have believed an hour earlier. "Oh, Sean," she said, turning back for a moment to call out to him. "I forgot to congratulate you. Nice work with the chandeliers!"

"Chandeliers?" He looked down at Cassandra, who had just discovered that, yes, it was possible to choke on one's own saliva. "What in hell is she talking about?"

"Later," she muttered, taking his hand and pulling him toward the parking lot. "We'll talk about it later. Right now, I want to go home, look up Smitty's phone number, then drive up to Burke. As he's the school janitor, he'll have a key. You see, I was looking at the wanted posters and different lists hanging on the walls of the police station, and I've gotten this idea...."

Seventeen

"So, seriously, Cassandra," Sean said as they drove away from Burke Senior High, back into Grand Springs, "have you considered a career in law enforcement? The FBI? The CIA? A cameo appearance in Clint Eastwood's next Dirty Harry movie, maybe?"

"Very funny," Cassandra shot back at him as he turned the corner on Seventh Street and headed down Maple. "All I did was employ a little common sense."

"Yes, I know. Which is something the local police didn't do." He smiled at her, really impressed by her brilliance. If the street weren't so crowded with traffic, and if he weren't the mature grown-up he wanted the world to believe he was, why, he might lean across the front seat and kiss her. Hell, he might just do it, anyway. He wasn't *that* old. He wasn't *that* responsible.

"We don't know that nobody thought of it, Sean," she corrected him, sounding once more the prudent professional. "For all we know, the police may have tried this months ago, with no success. But I'm glad you think it's worth taking the chance."

The "chance" they were taking had begun with a

ride back up the mountain road to Burke Senior High where Smitty had met them with his key to the front door. Once inside, Cassandra had used her own key to the principal's office and the file cabinet that contained information on every student enrolled at the school.

Part of that information was a list of every student who brought a car to school and used the school parking facilities. Each car had to be marked with a Burke sticker on the bumper, and each car had to be registered with the principal's office. A photocopy of the owner's card. The insurance information. The make of the car. The model. The year. The *color* of the car.

"Big Brother might not be watching everything we do these days," Sean had said as they'd paged through the information, "but he's getting closer all the time. And have you noticed how many kids are driving their own cars to school these days? Doesn't anyone ride the bus anymore? Why are two new buses penciled in for next year's operating budget? It sure doesn't look as if anyone is riding on them."

Cassandra had stuck a finger between two of the photocopied papers they had brought with them, carefully marking her place, and looked at him owlishly as she said, "You probably walked ten miles to school, each way, when you were young, right? Through rain and snow and dark of night. You know, like the postal service used to do? And that was after you got up at five to milk the cows and churn the butter."

Sean had decided he'd just been insulted. "I rode the bus every day until I graduated. No," he added,

"I take that back. I rode it until Charlie Hinkle got his license. Okay, so I didn't ride it every day. But I *did* use the bus the taxpayer's money provided for me."

"Exactly! You rode the bus until you could find another way to school. Those big yellow monsters are, like, ya know, totally *un*-cool," she'd said, mimicking the singsong cadence kids used. "Bumpy, too," she added quietly, going back to what she'd been doing. "Ah—here's another one!"

In the end, they had found eight white cars registered to Burke students. Three of those were driven by female students, two of those honor students, and the third belonging to a girl who had moved out of the district last May. Leaving five Burke students who were male—and Sean believed a male had to have been driving the car. It might have been chauvinistic of him, maybe even a blow to his fatherly pride, but he just couldn't picture his son being run off the road by a teenage girl.

Three of the boys had graduated just this June, and the other two were both in Jason's class.

Sean had decided to check out those two first, and they were now driving to the second house, the home of Brian Dunlevy, an honor student and the vice president of the class. Brian, Cassandra had told him, was also on the football team, the baseball team, and had been voted Student of the Month twice in the past three years.

Cassandra was sure Brian was as pure as the driven snow. Sean was prepared to hate the kid on sight.

After all, he'd *been* that kid, and he knew *he* hadn't been any purer than February slush.

"The Dunlevy house is just ahead, the second from the corner," Cassandra told him, her voice tense, her posture ramrod straight. "I can see a white car in the driveway, behind the station wagon."

"Nice house," Sean said, pulling over to the curb on the opposite side of the street and cutting the Blazer's engine. "You stay here, okay? I'll go have a look around."

"You'll be trespassing, you know," Cassandra pointed out, shivering in the predusk coolness. And out of nerves, he supposed.

"You going to turn me in?" Sean asked, grinning at her.

"Oh, would you just go and get it over with? Honestly, I'm beginning to think you're actually enjoying this."

"Better than a visit to the dentist."

"Worse than a splinter under my fingernail," Cassandra shot back.

"But better than a night of 'Baywatch' reruns."

"Who watches them the first time around?"

"Jason has every episode on videotape, all cataloged and numbered, if you must know. And you think you know all about teenagers? Uh-oh, too late!"

He was just about to open the door to the Blazer when the front door of the house opened and three teenage boys tumbled out, shoving and slapping at one another as they laughed and shouted and generally looked like they were about to head out to the local pizza parlor and a night of cruising the streets, looking for girls. At least that's how Sean could remember spending his summer evenings when he was their age.

He turned the key in the ignition. "Damn it. We'll just have to follow them. Is that Brian getting in the driver's seat?"

"Yes," Cassandra said, sighing. "Now, why would he have shaved his head like that? He didn't look like that in school when I saw him two weeks ago to tell him about his SAT scores. I really don't understand why anyone would do that to themselves unless they'd just joined the army or lost a bet, or something. I'm surprised his parents allowed it. Mrs. Dunlevy is president of the parent-teachers' organization, you understand. Her bake sale is always a resounding success. Such a lovely woman."

Sean had noticed that Brian Dunlevy was a big boy—tall, muscular. Not quite twice the size of his son, but definitely physically impressive. He put the Blazer in gear and followed the white car after it backed out of the driveway, heading toward Grand Springs Avenue. "Yeah, Cassandra, and Ted Bundy's mom probably made one hell of an apple pie. What does that have to do with anything?"

"Nothing, I guess. Should you be following them this closely? They might get suspicious."

"Only if they've thought about the possibility of somebody following them. Right now, I think the only thing they're trying to do is see how loud the radio can play without shattering every window on the block. Or maybe that's what they have in mind."

Cassandra sighed. "I don't like this. I don't like

this at all. I feel—I feel like a *stool pigeon!* These are my kids! Well, Brian is. I don't recognize those other two boys. Honestly, I don't know what's gotten into Brian lately. He acted as if he wasn't the least bit concerned about his—'' She stopped talking and turned to look out the window.

''Wasn't the least bit concerned about his *what*, Cassandra?'' Sean asked, sensing that she knew something she'd rather keep to herself.

''His SATs, if you must know,'' she told him, definitely reluctantly. ''He's always prided himself at being Burke's top student. I remember having to counsel him for a month after he got a B in his Modern Problems course last semester. You would have thought it was the end of the world! I guess that's because his brother and sister were both valedictorians when they were at Burke. That's a lot of pressure to put on a kid, you know? I mean, the whole family is so active in the school and all. They have one of those bumper stickers on their car. You know—My Child Is A Burke Honor Student.'' She shook her head. ''So much pressure. I don't know how kids stand it.''

Sean was beginning to think two and two might just make four. ''What was wrong with Brian's SATs, Cassandra? Did he bomb them?''

''No! Of course he didn't! Why, the only person in the junior class to score higher was—oh, Lord!'' She clapped her hands to her mouth, her eyes wide and frightened.

''You told Brian that Jason had the highest score?'' Sean asked, easing up on the gas as the white car slowed just ahead of a fast-food hamburger stand, preparing to pull onto the parking lot. "You did, didn't you? Why would you do that? I didn't think that was anyone's business except the individual student's. Although I wish I'd been informed of Jason's scores. It might have made life a little easier for the two of us."

"Scores aren't state secrets, Sean," Cassandra said a little testily. "And copies of the scores are sent to the student's home. I guess Jason must have picked up the mail that day, and then not told you about them, which was *his* decision, not mine. If you had called to ask about them, I most surely would have given them to you."

"Not to start an argument here, Cassandra, but how the hell was I supposed to call and find out about Jason's scores if I didn't know he had taken the damn test?"

Cassandra rolled her eyes. "Good point. I guess maybe I should start calling parents with the results, as a part of the overall postgraduation planning strategy for each student. Even if the parent has written the check to pay for the test, I can't assume that they know when their child has taken it. But I most certainly did *not* tell Brian about Jason's scores!"

"So why the shocked expression, Cassandra? Why the 'Oh, Lord!'"

She shook her head as if angry with herself, disappointed in herself. "I remember the day Brian was in my office. I was concerned about him, remembering how he'd reacted to the B in Modern Problems. I had the master sheet of SAT scores on my desk— and then Mr. Cummings knocked on the door and asked me to help him with a situation that had developed in the school cafeteria. Two girls were—well, let's just say that Jim Cummings isn't especially adept at dealing with two teenage girls who have just had a slapping contest over a boy, all right? I left the room for a few minutes, leaving Brian alone with the scores. I turned the paper over, of course, but that's all. I never should have done that. I should have shoved the results in my drawer before I left the room, but it didn't occur to me that he'd *look* at them—''

Sean pulled to the curb partway down the block from the fast-food restaurant and turned off the ignition. ''How long after that were the gym windows broken and Jason's notebook found at the scene?''

''About a week, I suppose,'' Cassandra said, opening the passenger-side door. ''Let's go have a look at that front bumper, all right? But I don't think I'm going to like what I see. Because,'' she said as they began walking down the sidewalk together, ''I also just remembered that Brian is not only the quarterback for Burke, but our place kicker, as well. Just as his older brother Zachary was three years ago, when I first came to Burke. So much pressure, Sean. Too damn much pressure!''

Sean could feel the muscles at the corners of his jaw beginning to throb. ''Don't try to make me feel sorry for this kid, Cassandra. It's not going to work. Jason and Becky could have been killed, remember?''

She slipped her hand into his, giving it a squeeze. ''I remember. I'm a guidance counselor, Sean, not Mother Teresa. If Brian is guilty, he has to be punished—as well as counseled. All I'm asking is that, if we do see something suspicious on the car, that you go to Detective Canfield with the information and don't try to talk to Brian yourself. That's all.''

Sean smiled down at her. ''Now who are you protecting, Cassandra? Brian—or me?''

''I'll get back to you on that, okay? Right after we've looked at the bumper and I have you safely back in the Blazer.''

''Hi, Jase,'' Sean said as he preceded Cassandra into the Frame family room, located toward the rear of the rambling three-story stone house on the outskirts of Grand Springs.

Cassandra had seen the outside of the house before, and liked what she'd seen, but the interior really surprised her. Cherry wood, Oriental rugs scattered over the hardwood floors—what she was certain of was an original Remington bronze of a cowboy on horseback in the place of honor on the huge round table in the foyer. Sean Frame might have grown up with next to nothing, but he certainly had good taste, and he most certainly had made up for lost time!

''Hi, Dad, Ms. Mercer,'' Jason said, hitting the mute button on the television remote control. ''Mom's upstairs, putting on some lipstick or something before she heads home, if you're looking for her. We called out for pizza and everything, so she's got to leave now to get home to Jesse. And I was just going out, after the Rockies bat in the bottom of the ninth. The score's been all tied since the sixth, but the bottom of their order is coming up, so it will probably go to extra innings unless somebody gets lucky and cranks one. I'll watch the rest over at Becky's. You don't mind if I go, do you? I promised I'd come sit with her awhile. Her parents are going to some banquet and she doesn't want to be alone.''

''I can't blame her,'' Sean said, motioning for Cassandra to take a seat in one of the chintz upholstered chairs that looked big enough, and comfortable enough, to swallow an elephant. ''After all, someone might come back to pay her a little visit, right? To make sure she keeps her mouth shut about your *accident?*''

Cassandra's heart broke for Jason, and she watched the color draining from his cheeks as his mother quietly came into the room and stopped beside her, slipping her hand into Cassandra's and giving it a squeeze.

''What's going on?'' Sally whispered. ''You could cut the tension in this room with a knife. Is everything all right? You found something out, didn't you. I thought you might be doing some investigating on your own, so I stuck around as long as I could. Is Jason in trouble?''

''Sean,'' Cassandra began hesitantly, ''why don't you just tell Jason what the two of us already found out on our own?''

Jason's eyes shifted from Cassandra, to his father, and then back again. ''What do you know? There's nothing to know. It was an accident. Just like I told Detective Canfield. That's all, an accident. Jeez— you'd think you guys were James Bond and…and… well, I don't know. Just let it go, okay?''

''We can't do that, Jase,'' Sean said, his voice low

and full of love. "We're your mom and dad, and Cassandra is your friend. Your very *good* friend, Jase, but I think you already know that. So why don't you tell us about it? About all of it. Starting with the day Brian Dunlevy planted your notebook outside the gym so that you'd take the fall for breaking the windows—and maybe not be allowed to try out for place kicker this fall."

"Windows? What's this craziness about broken windows? Jason would never do anything like that. Who's this Brian Dunlevy?" Sally whispered, squeezing Cassandra's hand again, harder this time. But she very prudently remained where she was and let Sean handle everything, and Cassandra's admiration for the woman doubled.

"You—you figured that out?" Jason wiped his hand across his mouth, looking caught between relief and fear. "How'd you figure that out? Brian said he and his buddies would break every last window at R & F if I told anybody, and then find a way to blame that on me, too. And you'd never believe I didn't do it. You think—you thought I hated you."

"Ah, Jase," Sean said, going over to his son and sitting down beside him, putting his arm around the boy's shoulders, giving him a rough, affectionate squeeze. "We still have a lot to work out, don't we. But we're going to start, okay? You, and me, and your mother—and Cassandra. If you'll let us? And tomorrow, with all of us beside you, you're going to go see Detective Canfield and tell him everything you know, because—well, let's just say that Cassandra and I might have cheated a little, so that our evidence was only good enough to bring to you, not to the police. Okay?''

''You'll do it, won't you, honey?'' Sally asked, leaving Cassandra's side and going down on her knees in front of Jason's chair. ''We'll be with you every step of the way. We promise.'' And then she drew her son into her arms, holding him tightly against her, just as if he were no older than her Jesse.

After a few moments, Jason raised his head from his mother's shoulder and looked over at Cassandra, who didn't really care that her cheeks were wet with tears and that her nose was running. She couldn't care about that at all. Because, for the first time in her life, she had been made part of a family. A wonderful, loving, accepting family—a family that took the good with the bad and forgave when forgiveness was needed, because it was a family grounded in love.

''Okay, Dad,'' Jason said, smiling at Cassandra. ''I'll do it. I mean, I wouldn't want to get you and Ms. Mercer in trouble, right?''

By Tuesday of the next week, it was all over. Brian Dunlevy had been released into his parent's custody, pending a hearing, and his two buddies, both of whom were over eighteen, had agreed to cooperate with the police in their investigation. The Dunlevys were shattered by the news, but Cassandra had already arranged for them to begin family counseling with a psychologist recommended by the school district.

The details weren't pretty. Brian had entered high school already carrying a load of responsibility and pressure on his shoulders in the form of his older siblings' performances at Burke before he arrived.

And the pressure had been too much, even though Brian was an intelligent boy. When he could no longer juggle his studies with his extracurricular activities, he had used his physical strengths as well as his popularity to convince other students to write reports for him, give him answers during tests. The B in Modern Problems had angered Brian because he felt it was due to the term paper he had badgered another student into writing for him—and that's when the real trouble had begun.

He'd run the student's car off the road in a fit of anger—the first incident Detective Canfield had told Sean and Cassandra about on the night of Jason's "accident."

Violence had worked once, and it worked a second time, with another student who had dared to say no to the great Brian Dunlevy when he ordered the boy to steal a test for him.

But Jason's SAT scores had put Brian over the edge. That, and learning that Jason, who had already displayed his kicking prowess on the school practice field during gym class, was actually—at the urging of the football coach who was also the gym teacher—going to try out for the football team in the fall.

Jason had known he was going to be blamed for the broken windows in the gymnasium before he had been called to the principal's office, because Brian had made a point of telling him—and of threatening him with more vandalism at Sean's business if he said anything.

With his father seeming more than ready to believe the worst of him, Jason had kept his mouth shut and taken the punishment the principal and Cassandra had devised for him. Because it wasn't all bad. At least he'd get to see Cassandra, who was just about the only grown-up he felt still might believe in him.

But things had changed since Sean and Cassandra had begun seeing each other. His dad was mellowing. Or maybe Jason was beginning to give his dad a chance. It didn't matter how it was happening, it was happening, and Jason could no longer stand knowing that his father thought he had broken the gym windows.

When he'd seen Brian and his friends that night, when he and Becky stopped at a teenage hangout for a soda, he'd taken the boy aside and told him that he was going to tell his father the truth.

As Sean told Cassandra, his son was doing the right thing, but his timing was way off. He should have come to Sean first, and told *him* what he planned, rather than confronting Brian, who had been desperate enough to chase after the Mercedes once it had pulled out of the lot and then ram the car. After all, violence had worked for Brian before this—why shouldn't it work again?

Jason had asked Cassandra if he could still do the reports that had been a part of his "punishment," because he felt he had been wrong to not have told his father what was happening, and Cassandra had agreed, assigning him one more report—this one on the importance of trust. He was doing his research at Sally's house, where he had gone to visit for a week, saying he thought it was time he got to know his new brother. "Mom says he does more than drool now, so that's cool," he'd told Cassandra before she and Sean waved goodbye to him as he drove away with Sally.

"I told him Jerry would hold his job open for the week," Sean told Cassandra as the two of them, arm in arm, turned back up the stone walkway leading to his front door. "He's got an *in* with the boss, you understand."

"That's nice," Cassandra said as he opened the door and motioned for her to precede him into the foyer. "Well, I'll just get my keys and head on home. Festus will be cutting me out of the will again if I don't feed him in the next hour or so."

Sean could sense that Cassandra was tense about something, but he didn't know what was bothering her. They hadn't been together much in the past few days, and they had never been alone. Did she think he didn't want her anymore, now that Jason was going to be all right? Was she out of her mind?

He took her hand, leading her into the den and then pulling her down on the soft cushions of the couch. Damn good purchase, this couch. Big. Soft. And practically impossible to get out of without help. She'd stay where he put her, because she really didn't have much choice.

Especially when he took hold of her hand and raised it to his lips, then held on to it in a way that had to tell her that she wasn't going anywhere.

"Festus—" she began as he reached over and began unbuttoning her blouse.

"Isn't going to starve in the next two hours," he finished for her, pulling her head against his shoulder. "Now, tell me what's going on?"

She tried to lift her head from his shoulder, but he wouldn't let her. "What's going on? *Nothing's* going on, Sean," she said, struggling against him for a moment, then giving up when she realized it was useless to fight him. "God, Frame, solve one small mystery and you think you're—you're—"

"James Bond?" he volunteered, relaxing his grip on her just slightly.

"Secret Squirrel!" she shot back, digging her elbow into his side and making a break for it when he yelped in surprise.

She took refuge behind one of the chairs, glaring at him evilly. "You think you're so smart, don't you? Well, you're not. And you know why? Because I was going to tell you, anyway." She slanted her gaze toward the door to the hallway. "Sometime."

"You're pregnant?" Sean felt his heart leap in his chest.

"No, I'm not *pregnant*," she shot back, and he saw the pain in her eyes. "Well, maybe I am. I don't know yet. It has only been a little over a week. Did you flunk biology, Sean? But that isn't what you really wanted to know, is it, because I know you want to know something. You want to know about *me,* don't you. I know all about Sally, and Jason, and your childhood, because you told me, but you know next to nothing about me, about my childhood, about the way I grew up, *how* I grew up. And it's killing you, isn't it? Well—you do want to know about it, don't you?''

Sean patted the cushion beside him, then sat back at his ease, waiting for her to come back to him. ''Well, if I do want to know, and you know I want to know, and I know you know that I want to know—'' he said, hesitating a moment, scratching his cheek, then rubbing his chin. ''Um, help me out here, will you, Cassandra? Where were we?''

She threw up her hands, rolling her eyes toward the ceiling. ''I *drank,* all right? The way I rebelled as a teenager was to drink. There—you happy now?''

Sean got to his feet and walked over to her, pulling her into his arms. ''I already sort of figured it might have been something like that, Cassandra. I guess I just wanted to hear you say it. Wanted you to trust me enough to tell me.''

''Damn you, Sean Frame,'' Cassandra whispered. ''You're something else, you know that?'' She burrowed against his chest. ''Yeah, well, I suppose that confession is supposed to be good for the soul, and all that sort of thing. God knows Jason has been happier than I ever remember seeing him.''

''Do you want to tell me about it? Because you don't have to, not really. It's just that, with my own background, it wasn't hard to figure out that you didn't have much of a childhood.''

She gave out a short snuffle of laughter that nearly broke his heart. ''Let's sit down, okay? Besides, I need a tissue. Maybe a box of tissues. I'm getting the front of your shirt all soggy.''

''Don't worry about my shirt, darling. It's weep-

and-wear,'' Sean assured her, but they did as she suggested, and he sat with his arm around her shoulder, waiting for her to blow her nose, to take a few deep breaths, to collect herself.

"I don't know why I'm telling you any of this," she said as she began shredding a tissue in her lap. "It's not like we're about to make some lifelong commitment to each other or anything."

"Want to bet?" Sean teased, pulling her closer. "We're getting married before the week is out, if I have my way, and within a month if you really say you need more time. I love you, Cassandra—which I probably should have told you first—but I had a feeling you wanted to tell me a few things before I got down on one knee and begged you to have me." He sighed, feeling something tight inside his body, deep inside his body, slowly beginning to uncoil after years spent wrapped tightly, protecting his heart.

This time he did allow her to raise her head, and she looked up at him with all the love in her eyes that he'd hoped, prayed, to see there. "I love you, too," she said, her bottom lip trembling. "And you don't have to ever be afraid of loving me. I'll never leave you, Sean. Never. Not even if you tell me to go."

"I know I've been a jerk, darling," he said, lowering his head to hers. "But I'm not that stupid."

It was a while—a long while—before Sean and Cassandra remembered to drive over to her house and feed the complaining Festus, after which they adjourned to the kitchen, sitting across the table from each other while Cassandra told him about her childhood.

"I'm not sure if I was wanted, or if I was an intellectual experiment my parents decided on fairly late in life—you know, a combining of extraordinary genes and their result," Cassandra said, then took another drink from the soda can she had opened a few moments earlier. "Either way, I knew early in life that I wasn't supposed to be like other children."

She smiled wanly. "They introduced me to algebra when I was four. Greek at five. I never had a Barbie doll, or a bike, but I did have my own do-it-yourself DNA model. Did I tell you that they pulled me out of school in the third grade to teach me at home? I didn't return to regular classes until I was in ninth grade and Mother was made head of her department, so that she was too busy to continue teaching me at home."

"Sounds like your childhood was a real barrel of laughs," Sean said, reaching his hand across the table to squeeze hers. He looked around the old-fashioned kitchen, the strictly functional kitchen. He thought about the rest of the house. "How did you stand it?"

She smiled again. "I had a great guidance counselor. Miss Quigley, who took a personal interest in me. She'd bring me in to her office, talk to me, let me talk. I'd go over to her house, sit in her kitchen while she made dinner for her family, help her weed her garden. We even went to movies together once in a while. Movies *without* subtitles. That's why I became a guidance counselor. Because of Miss Quigley. She even talked my parents into allowing me to go away to school, away from their influence. I loved her so much. She—she died in an automobile accident during my freshman year of college. My first college," she added quietly.

"And then you started to drink?"

Cassandra shook her head. "I started going to parties. You know, the classic cut loose and have fun stuff other kids do? But that didn't work out." Her smile cut into his heart. "Seems that kneeing the first guy who makes a pass at you is *not* the way to get invited back to fraternity parties."

"Prude," he said, squeezing her hand again.

"Definitely, or at least I was, until I ended up trapped inside a Jeep in the middle of a mud slide— with this handsome, thoroughly maddening man who seemed to always do his best to drive me crazy," she answered, drawing her hand free of his.

"I can do it again now, if you want. Drive you crazy, that is. And, I promise, I'll try to do my very best," Sean offered, not at all generously.

She laughed, as he'd hoped she would, easing some of the tension in the room. "Let me finish the story first, okay? If I don't say this now, I may never say it. I let my grades slip, even if I couldn't aspire to being a party girl, and that brought Mother and Dad down on me with both feet. They brought me home and enrolled me in the college they both taught at, made me live at home—and I damn near flunked out of school by the end of the first semester. It drove them wild! *I* drove them wild. And I loved it. Hey— at least I had their attention, right? So I was moved again, to another school."

"And the drinking?" Sean prompted, wanting the story over so that he could hold her, so that he could tell her how much he loved her in ways that would make her forget everything except that love.

"School three," she said, holding up her fingers. "I was enrolled too late to live on campus, so I had a room of my own, above a bar, no less. It was like some sort of omen, you know? I don't think I was an alcoholic, because I'd only been drinking for about four months, but I was definitely drunk when I got the call from Mother about my dad's first heart attack. She blamed me for causing it, of course, and she was probably right. I couldn't even get a bus home until I'd sobered up the next morning, and I didn't know if he'd be dead by the time I got to him." Tears sparkled in her eyes as she looked at Sean. "I haven't had a drink since."

He got up and came around the table, taking her hand so that she rose to her feet. "You aren't an alcoholic, Cassandra. Trust me on this. I think I might still hold the record for drinking the most beer in a single hour at my old fraternity. It's like you said, like Mrs. Quigley would have told you—you were rebelling."

"Acting out," she corrected him, smiling at him. "Or maybe just overreacting?" Then she looked around the kitchen, shaking her head. "I never changed a thing here after they died. I have no idea why, except that it never seemed to be *my* house, if you know what I mean? It was—is—their house."

"Yeah, I understand," Sean said, kissing her forehead. "And now it will be the house of whoever buys it. Because there's another house waiting for you, Cassandra, and it needs you to help make it into a home. For me, for Jason, and for our children when they come along. If you'll have me, that is.''

"You haven't gotten down on one knee yet, have you?'' Cassandra said, wiping away the last of her tears.

If he had his way, she'd never cry again. Although it might be nice if she shed a tear or two when he gave her the ring that he had in his pants pocket. ''You really want me on one knee?'' he asked, doing his best to look shocked.

''Would you rather be named chair of the committee to investigate my proposed introduction of a Marriage and Children course at Burke next year? I understand there's probably going to be quite a battle against the notion of the boys being made to wear vests that simulate the physical changes women undergo during pregnancy,'' she teased, the sparkle back in her eyes.

Sean had already dropped to one knee before she'd finished speaking.

Epilogue

Sean groaned as he lifted his head and looked at the clock on the night table, knowing it was time he got out of bed and took Cassandra home—before Jason returned from the multiplex. He rolled onto his side and picked up the remote control, pointing it toward the television in his bedroom, smiling as Cassandra grumbled under her breath as the late news came on.

"Turn that down a little, okay?" she mumbled, burying her head under the pillow.

"You'd think a modern woman would want to keep up on what's going on in the world," he teased, lowering the volume just a little, then turning it up again as a picture of Mayor Olivia Stuart was flashed on the screen. "Oh—look at this. They're doing another story on Olivia's murder."

"I may have to rethink this marriage business, if you're going to do this every night," Cassandra said, but she pushed the pillow away and sat up, brushing her hair out of her eyes. "I still can't believe anyone would have murdered that lovely woman. Have the police made an arrest?"

Sean leaned back against the headboard. "I don't think so. I just caught the tail end of the report and they've already gone on to another story. But it didn't sound like much more than a rehash of what we already know—that Olivia didn't die from a heart attack. We'll have to read about it in tomorrow's paper. Now they're doing another update on some of the babies born during the storm. The preemie we read about the other day, and a set of twins.'' He turned to look at Cassandra. ''Cute, huh? Twins would be nice.''

''Don't even *think* it!'' she retorted. ''We'll just do them one at a time, if you don't mind.''

Sean didn't believe he needed any more of an invitation. Turning off the television, he leaned over, partially lowering his body onto Cassandra's. ''I don't mind the extra effort if you don't, darling.''

''Idiot!'' she said, halfheartedly slapping at his hand as it found its way beneath the hem of her short gown. ''Besides, I thought you said you had to go in to work early tomorrow if you're going to be able to block out enough free time to make an honest woman of me before we start setting a bad example for Jason. Although living in sin is rather exciting for this old maid schoolteacher prude.''

''Former prude,'' Sean corrected her, remembering her rather daring lovemaking of less than an hour ago. ''But you're right. It has been a great two weeks, but I do have a lot of work to catch up on at the office. Especially now that Grace isn't coming back.''

Cassandra wrinkled her forehead in question. ''Grace? Do you mean Miss Finley, your dragon of a secretary? Where did she go? Why isn't she coming back?''

Sean slid his hand higher, splaying his fingers over

Cassandra's flat belly. "Didn't I tell you?" he asked, trying not to laugh. "I gave her a two week vacation the same time I started my own. I got a fax from her this morning, from San Diego. She's quit."

"Quit? But she seemed so dedicated to you."

"Oh, she loves me with all her heart and soul and wants to work for me forever," Sean said, wondering how long it would take before he'd have Cassandra's nightgown off her once more. "But, seeing as she capped off her vacation by eloping to Vegas with a podiatrist and will be living in San Diego, she thought it might be too much of a commute. Now, come here, woman. Let's talk babies—and about that lovely blue stick you showed me this morning."

"You don't *talk* babies, darling," Cassandra said, moving suggestively beneath him. "I don't know how you ever passed biology, truly I don't. But that's all right. I'll tutor you."

"Bet I get straight As," Sean mumbled against her breast. "I'm a real quick learner."

*   *   *   *   *

36 Hours

When disaster turns to passion

continues with

OOH BABY, BABY

by Diana Whitney,
also available in April

Here's an exciting preview…

Ooh Baby, Baby

June 6th

Outside, the rain pummeled the thin windowpanes. Thunder rumbled. Lightning cracked. Inside, the silence of her heart was deafening. And so very, very lonely.

Peggy Saxon shifted on the worn sofa to massage the small of her back. It didn't help. The nagging throb simply wouldn't go away. She heaved her pregnant bulk sideways, seeking a semicomfortable position. On the radio, a male voice announced new road closures due to mud slides. Phone lines were holding, but the power company still had no estimate as to when electricity would be restored. A state of emergency had been declared. Grand Springs, Colorado, was under siege.

Another flash. A loud, overpowering roar. Then the rumbling softened into silence.

Peggy blinked into the darkness, and grabbed the flashlight at her side. She followed the light toward the front door, then veered left to aim the beam through the window and check the front porch—or rather, what was left of it. The dilapidated decking had been crushed by an enormous pine, now wedged against her front door. Judging by the angle, she suspected that the other half of the duplex had born the brunt of the damage. Fortunately, the unit was vacant, which meant her nearest neighbor was a quarter mile away.

A grinding pain suddenly ripped her belly like a buzz saw, doubling her over. She had no breath to cry out, but her mind screamed for her. Fear surged victorious. She was in labor.

And she was alone.

"Dispatch to unit six. Travis…are you there?"

Travis Stockwell ducked into the cab, knocked his hat off on the door frame, and swore as his prized Stetson landed in the mud.

The raspy female voice boomed with familiar agitation. "Unit six, respond. Respond, dadgummit."

"All right, already. This is unit six."

A long-suffering sign crackled over the line. "We have an emergency relay from 9-1-1 dispatch. Pick up is at five-six-six-two Rourke Way."

Travis was familiar with the street, a rutted two-lane cutting a rural swath around the outskirts of town. He jotted the address on a scratch pad affixed to the dash. "I'll be there in ten."

He picked up his hat, hung a U-turn, stomped the accelerator, and sped away.

Breathe, breathe, breathe.

Short, shallow breaths. Or maybe take a deep breath and hold it. Peggy couldn't remember. Dear Lord, she couldn't remember. Squeezing her eyes shut, she willed herself to focus on what she'd learned. Short breaths. Yes, she was sure now. Short breaths during labor, deep breaths during crowning, when it was time to push.

To push. Oh, God. It was too soon, Peggy thought frantically. She wasn't due for three weeks. She wasn't ready to give birth, not ready at all....

Where the hell was that cab?

The thought occurred that there was no way for her to get out through the front door, no way for anyone else to get in. But Peggy couldn't worry about that now because a vise-like tightness was working its way from the base of her spine around her belly.

Breathe, breathe, breathe.

The pain swelled, twisted, sliced like a dull blade. Tears sprang to her eyes. She curled forward, wanted to scream, and imagined a hundred innovative ways for the ex-husband who'd abandoned her to die ugly.

Travis pulled onto the dirt shoulder behind a clunky old sedan and fervently hoped he was at the wrong address. Anyone left inside that crushed structure needed an ambulance, not a cab. Closer examination revealed that, except for the porch, the dwelling itself seemed to be relatively unscathed. Shading his eyes, he squinted and saw the door was undamaged, but completely blocked by the tree trunk. He cupped his mouth and shouted. "Conway Cab. Anyone in there?" A movement behind one of the windows caught his eye, and he thought he saw a shadow inside the room. Before he could focus, the shadow seemed to collapse, melt in upon itself, and was gone.

Ducking into the wind, Travis circled back toward the rear of the old duplex. A five-foot wooden fence creaked against the wind. He hoisted himself up and over, wincing as he dropped into the yard. Doc had warned that ribs fractured that badly were slow to heal. Slow? Hell, that wasn't the half of it. Travis longed for the cheering crowds and bellowing livestock of the rodeo. Rawhide rasping his palms. The pungent smell of animalistic power, of sweating victory and bloody defeat. But just a few more weeks and he'd be back on the circuit, back where he belonged.

After a quick glance around, he strode to the back door, peered through the mullioned window and tapped on the glass. When there was no response, he frantically rattled the knob. It was locked, so he took a step back and kicked in the door. In less than a heartbeat, he knelt beside a woman who was curled on her side, making strange hissing sounds through her teeth.

He laid a tentative hand on her shoulder. "Ma'am?"

She opened her eyes, huge pools of emerald terror in a colorless face.

Travis's breath backed up his throat. "It's all right," he muttered with considerably more confidence than he felt. "You're going to be fine, ma'am, just fine."

Her eyes widened, then squinched shut. To his shock, she formed her lips into an O and began to pant. He blinked and noticed the bulge of her abdomen long before the reason for it struck him. When it did, he danged near went into shock.

"Oh, no," he murmured, utterly transfixed by the realization. "No, no, ma'am, you can't do this…not now. Please, lady—"

Her cheeks flexed with each quick puff.

"Oh, Lordy—"

Puff, puff, puff.

"Ma'am, please stop. This just really isn't a good time. Can't you put this off for a while? I mean, this is a really, really bad time to have a baby.…"

♥™ SILHOUETTE
SENSATION®

ON-SHELF NOW

BADGE OF HONOUR Justine Davis

Trinity Street West

Police chief Miguel de los Reyes had worked with Sergeant Kit Walker for years, but never this closely. Now he found himself looking for excuses to be near her, to touch her. But would giving in to passion jeopardize their case and prevent them bringing a dirty cop to justice?

A HUSBAND WAITING TO HAPPEN
Marie Ferrarella

Twelve years ago, Sloane Walters had thought of Caroline Masters as nothing more than a friend and he had pledged his love to another woman. But now he was raising two boys alone and time had changed a lot of things—including the way he looked at Caroline…

RETURN TO SENDER Merline Lovelace

Nothing exciting ever seemed to happen to post office worker, Sheryl Hancock. At least not until she noticed some mysterious postcards and stumbled into the middle of detective Harry MacMillan's investigation. Now Harry wanted to grill her day and night about what she knew. Or did he have something else in mind for their time together?

SHADOW'S FLAME Alicia Scott

The man named Shadow had crept swiftly and silently through the dense Burmese jungle to rescue Riley McDouglas from a wrecked plane. Riley knew him to be a mercenary, a man whose grey eyes hid deadly secrets. But he was her only hope!

SILHOUETTE
SENSATION®

COMING NEXT MONTH

ROARKE'S WIFE Beverly Barton

The Protectors

Heiress Cleo McNamara desperately needed a husband and a bodyguard.
Security expert Simon Roarke bravely took *both* jobs—for a limited
time. But when his contract was up, could he really leave Cleo in danger
especially when she was carrying his child?

WHILE SHE WAS SLEEPING Diane Pershing

Heartbreaker

Carla Terry led a very mundane life until she woke up one morning in a
stranger's arms. She could remember a night of incredible passion but
that was *all* she could remember. Fortunately, cop Nick Holmes
promised to stay by her side until she found out who was playing games
with her life!

PARTNERS IN PARENTHOOD Raina Lynn

Jill Mathesin was a pregnant bride and she was marrying the man she
loved. But Mason Bradshaw was only marrying her because of the
baby—*his* baby, conceived one wonderful, reckless night. What had
happened to make this man so wary, and could Jill hope to win his heart?

UNDERCOVER COWBOY Beverly Bird

Secret agent Jack Fain had chased his arch-enemy around the world...to
a ranch in the middle of nowhere. Jack's job description didn't include
falling for ranch owner, Carly Castagne. Personal involvement could
only raise the stakes of the game. But soon protecting her became as
essential to him as catching the assassin.

HELEN R. MYERS

Come Sundown

In the steamy heat of Parish, Mississippi, there is a new chief of police. Ben Rader is here to shape up the department, and first on the list is the investigation of a mysterious death.

But things are not what they appear to be. Come Sundown things change in Parish…